"It seems to me," Georgia said, "that we are dealing with a most

Qu...

If ...
li...
th...
wa...
th... ...ovington. It was an
od... ...ful sensation.

M...e more so by what Matthew saw hiding behind Georgia's eyes—an admiration for the recklessness that came close to affection for the dashing hero.

But the Bandit was reckless. Matthew Covington could not be. Dashing midnight bravery was a luxury for imaginary men, not Covingtons.

Still, he would do it again. To watch her talk of it with that look on her face. To know that she held a part of him—even an invented part—in such esteem. It was enough.

Books by Allie Pleiter

Love Inspired Historical

Masked by Moonlight #9

Steeple Hill Books

Bad Heiress Day
Queen Esther & the Second Graders of Doom

Love Inspired

My So-Called Love Life #359
The Perfect Blend #405

ALLIE PLEITER

Enthusiastic but slightly untidy mother of two, Allie Pleiter writes both fiction and non-fiction. An avid knitter and non-reformed chocoholic, she spends her days writing books, drinking coffee, and finding new ways to avoid housework. Allie grew up in Connecticut, holds a BS in Speech from Northwestern University, and spent fifteen years in the field of professional fundraising. She lives with her husband, children and a Havanese dog named Bella in the suburbs of Chicago, Illinois.

ALLIE PLEITER

Masked by Moonlight

Steeple Hill®

Published by Steeple Hill Books™

STEEPLE HILL BOOKS

Steeple Hill®

ISBN-13: 978-0-373-82789-3
ISBN-10: 0-373-82789-X

MASKED BY MOONLIGHT

This edition published by arrangement with Steeple Hill Books.

www.SteepleHill.com

Printed in U.S.A.

For now we see in a mirror, darkly; but then face to face: now I know in part; but then shall I know fully even as also I was fully known. But now abideth faith, hope, love, these three; and the greatest of these is love.

—1 *Corinthians* 13:12–13

For Georgia
Dream big dreams, little one

Acknowledgment

I was blessed to have loads of great help on this book, and any blame for historical errors you find should lay squarely on my own shoulders, not with any of my fine sources. Eileen Keremitsis lent tireless and creative help in general research and fact finding. Howard Mutz and Gena Egelston dug up hotel details, while the Golden Gate Hotel served as my home away from home in San Francisco. Andrew John Conway taught me to wield a whip and made valuable book recommendations. It's a given that I'd be sunk without the ongoing support of my family, my agent Karen Solem, my editor Krista Stroever, and the wonderfully supportive ranks of Windy City RWA, Chicago North RWA, and the local and national branches of American Christian Fiction Writers. As always, the highest credit goes to my God, who continues to take me on the most amazing journey of all.

Chapter One

San Francisco
1890

Set up, turn, release.

The whip sliced cleanly through the night. Without the expected crack.

Matthew Covington pulled the whip behind him again, blowing out an exasperated breath. *That's twice you've missed.* The moonlight and shadows should have eased his overwrought spirit. He checked the last few inches of the whip, making sure they were intact. He knew they would be. His own frayed concentration was at fault here, not his whip. *Come now, man. Gather your wits.* He rolled his shoulders and flexed his fingers around the hilt. *Why still so tense?* He'd doffed his collar and waistcoat. Fled that dark, fussy office where his duty to be the respectable guardian of the Covington family honor accosted him at every tight turn. Surely out here, in shirtsleeves, in the noisy darkness of unfamiliar San Francisco, Matthew could find the space he craved.

After a moment's consideration, he put the whip down and flipped open the latch on a long wooden box at his feet. Moonlight caught the sword's edge as he lifted it from the dark blue velvet. *Whhhish.* Matthew listened for the blade's soothing whisper. Although a formidable opponent with any of his weapons, he cared little for combat. He was drawn to the marriage of tool and muscle, the form and stretch of putting the weapon through its courses. The exertion. The application of skill. *Whoosh.* Matthew's whole body seemed to exhale as he sent the sword curving through the cool darkness.

He wasn't satisfied. Fencing often eased his knotted shoulders, but he'd just had a long, excruciating day, and it simply wasn't enough. Tonight, his tension needed the whip's power more than the sword's grace, and Matthew's hand returned to the whip's hilt seemingly on its own.

"I told you!" A sudden voice broke the quiet. Two figures burst into the end of the alley. Matthew froze, glad he'd replaced his white lawn shirt with a darker one as a last-minute precaution.

"It ain't worth nothin', I reckon," one said.

"Lemme open it." The larger man bumped his companion aside and reached into a small bag.

"I git half, remember."

"You get a third. Aw, will you look at this?" The big one held up a handful of coins, obviously disappointed.

"You pick a runt to rob and expect to get gold? We ain't gonna get anywhere if you keep—" A stack of boxes fell over as someone new ran into the alley.

Someone small.

"Gimme that back!" the thin voice panted. It was a boy—no more than ten years old, from the looks of him.

Matthew's chest constricted. His fingers tightened around the whip. *Covington, stay out of this.* He backed up against the wall.

But not before taking a half-dozen silent steps toward the action.

"Aw, looky here, what followed us." The pair flanked the boy, each man pushing up his sleeves.

Nothing needs saving, Covington. Certainly not by you.

"It's mine. I want my money back!" The boy put up a pair of tiny, heroic fists.

Don't don't don't don't don't...

The large man dangled the bag out of the boy's reach, taunting him. "Life ain't fair, runt. Better learn it now. Unlessen you're in a hurry to meet your maker."

"Give it to me!" The lad lunged at the smaller of the men, who caught him easily. Matthew glimpsed the glint of a blade against the boy's throat.

How could he not?

Matthew took four huge strides, readying the whip as he went. Silently, staying in the building's shadow, he lifted his arm. *Set up. Turn.* He sent the long arc of leather hissing through the air, to crack angrily half a foot to the right of the boy's captor. The knife was too close to the lad's throat to chance it, but the crack had the effect needed. As the burly man yelped and flinched, Matthew sent his whip out again, this time around the small bag.

He gave a precise yank, sending the purse sailing into the air to land a few feet in front of him.

"What the…?" The other man spun in Matthew's direction, his own blade raised. At least the lad knew enough to bolt out of his captor's grasp the second he flinched.

Matthew drew a breath to hiss something threatening when his brain cautioned him to stay silent. His British accent would give him away in a heartbeat. Or at least make him easier to identify. Instead, he sank as far into the shadow as he could and pulled the whip back a third time. This time it wrapped around the legs of the second man and pulled him down on top of his companion.

Why didn't the boy run to safety? Matthew remembered the bag. He considered throwing it to the lad, but that would force him to step into the light again, and the men were already scrambling to their feet. When Matthew noticed the pair lacked guns or holsters—a rare but fortunate circumstance—he calmly drew the revolver from his side. The unmistakable click of the hammer stopped them cold. He let the silver tip of the gun catch the moonlight, and the pair promptly fled, disappearing around the corner.

Exhaling, Matthew holstered the gun and picked up the bag. The boy stood gaping at him with wide eyes. Matthew tossed the bag to the lad, who was too busy straining to see into the shadows to catch it.

There was a long pause. Matthew held his tongue, but finally nudged the purse with his foot.

"Oh. Uh-huh." Still staring, the boy crouched down and groped for it.

Matthew forced himself to focus on coiling his whip. When he looked up, the child was gone.

Then, just as he turned back toward his box, Matthew heard it—the long wail of a running boy calling, "*Thanks*, mister!"

If Georgia Waterhouse was going to save the world one child at a time, someone had beaten her to it.

At least as far as the scrappy newsboy before her was concerned. Snapped from the very jaws of death, to hear him tell it. And tell it he had. He was on his fourth rendition of the morning, the pertinent details growing with every repetition as they sat in the Grace House Mission hallway.

"I thought you said he had one whip last time, Quinn. Now he's wielding two." Georgia smiled and put down the package of clothes she was wrapping. She knelt in front of the boy, tight as they were for space as they moved packages from the hallway into the mission linen closet.

She handed the boy a shirt to hold. "You know, Quinn, this is a pretty tall tale. Men don't just appear out of the shadows with whips and guns in the middle of the night to save boys." She knit her brows together as she reached behind her for another garment. "And what was it you were doing out so late, in any case? Did anyone know where you were?"

He shot her a look that said she didn't know anything. "*Everyone* knew," he said, with the whine of someone who felt he was stating the obvious. "I *always* run back to Uncle Hugh with the coins from the newsstand."

"At three in the morning?" Georgia pivoted around to pack up the shirts she held with the ones she took back from Quinn. The mission was running out of storage space. Again.

"No, most times it's closer to two."

She sighed. The fact that ten-year-old newsboys were ferrying money through back alleys at three in the morning was exactly why God had asked her to save the world—or at least San Francisco's corner of it—here through Grace House Mission.

"You know, Quinn, it'd be easy to make up a tale that some man saved you and your money from those robbers, especially if you thought people might admire you if you did. God—and I—would rather you tell the truth."

"I *am* telling the truth. *God* knows that, anyhow!"

Georgia pointed to another pile of clothes and switched tactics. "Hand me those, will you, please? I'm simply saying that it's all right to make up stories. I do it all the time. But passing them off as real is another thing altogether."

Quinn's eyes took on a nasty edge. "I *knew* no one'd believe me." He threw the pile onto the hallway floor. "Prob'ly not even God, and *He* should know better." Disgusted, he tore off around the corner, leaving the clothes scattered on the floor behind him.

Georgia heard Reverend Bauers call out down the hall as he dodged out of Quinn's angry path. The clergyman appeared at Georgia's side a second later, looking down the hall after Quinn's exit.

"Told you the tale of his midnight hero, has he?"

Georgia gathered up the clothing. "Four times. It got more heroic with every telling."

Bauers chuckled. "How many whips in your version?" He was a jovial soul of solid German stock, and Georgia was very fond of him and the work he'd done here at Grace

House. The struggling "South of the Slot" neighborhood—named for its position south of the cable car line—was far better off for his efforts.

"I stopped him at two."

"It got to the point where I thought our hero would resort to cannon fire in my set of renditions," he grunted as he bent his considerable frame to gather the last of the shirts. "Oh well, I can't say as I blame the boy."

Georgia eyed him. "Telling lies?"

"More like exaggerating, I'd say. I believe *someone* got Quinn out of a scrape last night. Whether or not he wielded a trunkful of weaponry, I am not so sure. But boys need heroes, and San Francisco is in painfully short supply."

Chapter Two

"Georgia, you always get these kinds of ideas after you've been to Grace House."

Georgia stared at her brother. They sat talking over breakfast in the family dining room. The sun had overpowered the morning fog, to produce a victorious wash of bright light. Unlike the estate's massive formal dining hall, this was a warm and comfortable room. Georgia had seen to its welcoming palette of honey-colored wood, gold and tan wallpaper, with a few hints of green and burgundy in various accents. She loved that the petit point chair cushions were their late mother's needlework. That the impressive gold candlesticks and clock on the fireplace mantel had been a favorite of their late father's. Even though they were long gone, this dining room was one of the places she most felt her parents' presence. Perhaps that's why she had chosen to launch her extraordinary plan over breakfast here.

"That place has cost me thousands of dollars in your

brand of philanthropy. They've got you hoodwinked," her brother was saying.

Georgia gathered strength from the room around her and silently held her ground. Or, as she liked to think of it, she held ground for God.

Stuart finally looked up from his paper. "You're not serious."

"I am." With one hand she instinctively gripped the cushioned arm of her chair, as if her mother's needlework would support her cause.

"Peach, I can't just run something like that in the *Herald,*" said her brother, who often called her Peach, especially when being difficult. "You know that."

"You run whatever you please in that paper, Stuart. Facts or no facts." Georgia knew she had him there. Stuart Waterhouse ran a highly successful but highly disreputable paper.

"Peach," he moaned at her display of determination, "be reasonable. We've already had a Black Bandit Bart. People aren't going to believe that some man with the same name as that stagecoach robber has suddenly sprung up to play the noble hero. They aren't going to believe it *at all.* It's *fiction.*"

Fiction. How funny of him to use such a term. She wondered what he called half of his paper's contents, since Georgia knew the term "fact" hardly applied. Quite clearly, Stuart viewed fiction as something beyond his dealings, even though Georgia imagined half of San Francisco might think otherwise.

"I know very well what it is. And believe me, Stuart, if I had a set of good deeds for your reporters, I'd tell you. But, as you so often point out, this city seems steeped in bad news. And you gave Black Bandit Bart a lot of coverage, so why not a new Black Bandit?"

Stuart rolled his eyes. "Oh come now, Georgia, times aren't as bad as all that."

"Aren't they? Have you visited Grace House? Seen what kind of people come there asking for help? Things are going from bad to worse lately. You know it. I worry that you thrive on it, for goodness' sake." She reached for the morning's edition of the *Herald,* which lay on the table between them. The cool black-and-white newsprint stood out against the honey-toned wood that surrounded them.

Georgia unfolded the paper and held it up to her brother. "I don't see a piece of good news in here, Stuart. Can you show me even one story?"

He evaded her challenge, as she knew he would. "I'm not going tit for tat with you on this." He rose and walked to the window, slipping his hands inside the pockets of his crisp gray trousers. He was a fastidious dresser, her brother. He always looked sharp and strong, his meticulously tailored coat rarely unbuttoned. "Write all the stories you like, tell tales to your heart's content," he said, gazing out the window. "Just don't ask me to run them in the *Herald.*"

The servants brought in breakfast, interrupting the exchange. The siblings ate in silence, he thinking he'd ended the conversation, she regrouping for another attempt.

When he'd finished the last of his eggs, Georgia slid the paper over to his side of the table once more. She would not back down. Not again. "We don't have any good news, Stuart. We're going to have to make our own. Fiction reminds people of what *could* be. Stories touch their hearts. This city isn't suffering from a lack of facts. Folks already have more than enough facts to fill their heads. It's suffering from a lack of heart. A lack of faith. Stories reach that part of us."

Stuart's expression told her she was speaking about things he neither understood nor valued. He ran his empire, and cared little for lingering over breakfast to discuss San Francisco's moral failings.

He didn't concern himself with the citizens' hearts or souls.

Their wallets, however, commanded his full attention.

Georgia looked at the candlesticks, massive and ornate. Her father had brought them back from a trip because he'd felt they caught one's eye. They were, in fact, the first thing anyone noticed when entering the room. She needed to catch her brother's eye, then, and put this in terms he could appreciate. She altered the tone of her voice.

"If there's one thing you know, Stuart, it's how to give your readers what they want." She handed him a small stack of handwritten pages. "Read this. Just read it once, that's all I'm asking." She sent up a prayer that he would do so. "See what those famous instincts of yours tell you about what people might think of this."

Stuart reached for a piece of toast and glared at her.

She did her best to glare back. *Lord, please let him read it. Only You can do this.*

Slowly, Stuart's hand moved toward the pages. She straightened her spine, trying to look as if she'd never leave the breakfast table until he granted her request. If the sun could conquer the fog this morning, she could stand up to Stuart.

He took hold of the pages while biting into his toast.

Georgia waited. *Show him, Lord. Let him see it. See what I see.*

She studied her brother's face as he began to read. After a paragraph or two, Stuart stopped chewing. He let out a little humming sound as he turned the page.

"It's fine work, but I..."

"You ought to have thought of this yourself, Stuart. You ought to have *written* it yourself. It would do you a world of good to pen something that might actually be categorized as...uplifting."

Stuart dismissed the idea with a snort. "I haven't any talent for *this* sort of thing." He put down the toast, half-eaten, and emptied his coffee cup instead. "'Uplifting' doesn't sell."

Georgia tried out her newfound glare once more. "But you know this will sell. And don't try to deny it—I see it on your face. Everyone needs a hero. And if they need one bad enough, he doesn't even have to be real. That little boy at Grace House made up his own personal hero so he'd believe he had someone looking out for him. So he could believe that good might just conquer evil, after all. Hold up a little piece of good for once, Stuart. It won't hurt you. And won't cost you a dime."

Her brother was right in one respect: he *couldn't* have written it. There was nothing ideological about Stuart. He'd built a fortune on his keen grasp of the public's insatiable hunger for news. *His* brand of news. Sharp, eye-catching, unabashedly partisan news. In all honesty, her brother's outlandish character sold as many papers as his headlines. Stuart Waterhouse wasn't exactly known for his respect of facts, but his opinions were the stuff of legend.

Well, she could be a legendary Waterhouse, too. And

Georgia knew, just as God did, that the public's appetite for something good was just as strong as its craving for slander.

"Run it, Stuart. One installment. As a favor to me."

"Georgia, I'm not—"

"Please, Stuart. For me."

A wry smile crept across his face, and she knew she had him. "Oh, very well, then, I'll run it."

Thank you, Father!

"On two conditions."

Well, if she hadn't known that was coming, it was her own fault. She should have guessed there'd be *conditions.*

Stuart held up one finger. "Pen name."

"But..."

"*Male* pen name," he asserted.

So the victory goes to a George, not a Georgia, hmm? She rolled the idea over in her mind and decided that the prospect might be acceptable. As unconventional as Stuart could be, even *he* knew that writing as a man was a safer idea. Still, would it be deceitful? Georgia looked at the *Herald,* lying crisp and bright on the table between them. Tomorrow's paper would contain her story. *Her story.* Even "George" couldn't dampen the thrill in that. She waited for some sense of a heavenly warning, but none came. Just the joy of seeing the story come to light. That was confirmation enough for now.

She nodded.

"And second, speaking of favors, I'm having someone over to dinner tomorrow night...."

That one Georgia had seen coming a mile off.

Chapter Three

"And in that instant, the Black Bandit flung himself onto his gleaming mount and rode off into the night. In his wake, he left his injured enemy slumped at the sheriff's feet. And behind them, the huddled group of children, astounded and grateful. Justice had prevailed in the bravery of a soft-spoken man whom no one could name."

"Well, hang me, Peach, you really can turn a phrase. Astounding." Stuart had actually interrupted his breakfast to read her the Bandit's debut installment. "How does it feel, *Mr. George Towers,* to have your dashing hero introduced to the world?"

Georgia couldn't deny her joy. Nor could she deny the blatant admiration in Stuart's voice as he read the piece. It was identical to the handwritten words he'd read yesterday, but the man's love affair with ink and newsprint was overwhelming. It struck Georgia that her Bandit was her brother's exact opposite: larger than life, just like him, but a man of impeccable heroic morals, where Stuart was a man of… Perhaps it was more polite to say his morals were rather in question.

Her Bandit was a shamelessly inspirational hero. A dark and brooding champion. Georgia had taken the seed of an idea planted by Quinn and his fantastic tale, woven in a touch of Robin Hood, and then spiced it with the distinct grandiosity of the American West. She envisioned him like King David in his glory: distant and handsome, strong, compelled by an unshakable code of justice. Like all good heroes, he had the knack of sweeping in just when all hope seemed lost.

"Here's the way I see it, Peach. Do you notice where it's placed? On the back page here? I've posted your story right where someone else can see it while a man reads the paper." Stuart held up the issue in a classic pose, then peeked above it at Georgia. "You can read about your hero while I read the other pages. I see wives across San Francisco catching a glimpse of our Bandit while their husbands scan the business column. Brilliant, don't you think? Our man George ought to be a hit by week's end."

Georgia eyed her brother. Why did it surprise her that he was managing to capitalize on this? Only Stuart could take something so noble and turn it into a way to sell more papers. Not to mention his sudden partnership in the idea. *Our* Bandit? *Our* man George?

"It's how Dickens got his start, you know," offered Stuart in response to her look. "Serialized in the dailies."

Georgia was not Dickens. She wasn't even sure how she felt about being George Towers. She'd prayed over it for hours after her agreement, waiting for God to put His foot down and end the charade. Instead, she continued to feel as though God had opened this window and wasn't in any hurry to shut it. It was an idea born of good intentions, given directly to her by the Almighty—or so it felt. But it was still a deception of sorts. One couldn't ignore Stuart's manipulation of her, nor their partnered manipulation of the public's imagination.

But oh, there it was. Sprung to life in the *Herald*'s wonderfully immortal ink. Sparking some hope in the troublesome world that was San Francisco these days. She thought of the spark in Quinn's eyes.

"Peach? You've got that far-off look again. I always worry when you look like that. I'm not always fond of what shows up afterward."

Georgia set her teacup down with a resolute clink and stared straight into Stuart's inquiring eyes. "Stuart, thank you."

"My pleasure. For what?"

"For being important."

He merely returned her stare, and she could watch him resign himself to the oddities of his sister. And that's precisely how Stuart viewed Georgia's faith: as one of her oddities. "Speaking of my vast importance—not to mention that favor you owe me—Matthew Covington's coming to dinner tonight."

"Covington? The dry goods company?" Georgia surveyed the flowers brought in for tonight's dinner table. They were almost right. Not enough bright colors. The gardener was forever forcing pastels on her.

"He's that English fellow I was telling you about," replied Stuart, plucking a blossom from the center of the cuttings for his own lapel. "The flesh-and-blood heir to that dry goods company. He's here doing the family duty, showing up to play at keeping his eye on things."

"And, of course, you asked him to dinner."

Stuart launched into a chorus from Gilbert and Sullivan.

"Because he is an Englishman!
And he himself has said it, and it's greatly to his credit,
For he is an Englishman.
He i-i-i-s an E-e-e-ennn-glish-man!"

Just before he ducked around the corner, Stuart looked back at her. "He's vastly important and very wealthy. I want him to have a grand time while he's here. That's where you come in. Fire up your charms, Peach, I want the man dazzled."

Oh yes, with Stuart there was always a deal.

Matthew eyed his valet as the old man held up the remains of a newspaper. Pages had been sliced to ribbons. "You do know, sir," said Thompson wearily, "that a large portion of Englishmen *sleep* at night?"

"Yes, Thompson," he replied, finishing up his collar, "I'm well aware of that. But no one has yet expired from a bout of sleeplessness, so I gather I'm safe to live another day." He shrugged into the coat Thompson held out, offering the most challenging look he could muster. The old man merely opened the door and handed Matthew a thick file, looking as if he might nap the minute Matthew left the room.

"Remember your dinner engagement at Stuart Waterhouse's home this evening. Shall I order up a double set of tonight's papers, sir, so you can read them *and* duel them?"

Try as he might, Matthew couldn't think of a clever enough response. His valet was always getting the last word. Probably what kept him alive all these years.

As Matthew boarded the carriage bound for the Covington Enterprises offices, Matthew's family duty spread before him like a dull column of orderly figures. He merely had to inspect what was presented and tally up the sum. There seemed so little art to it. Like the predictable shot of a rifle. None of the arc or parry he found in the foil or the whip. Pull. Aim. Shoot. Obey.

"How are you finding San Francisco, Mr. Covington?"

"Lovely, thank you."

"I'm glad to hear you're enjoying your stay." Miss Waterhouse gave him a charming smile. "San Francisco is not…everyone's taste," she continued. "I'm afraid we've not quite grown into our big-city shoes."

"What my sister means is that we're still a bit rough around the edges, Covington," interjected Stuart.

"Not at all, Waterhouse." Matthew forced his gaze away from the man's sister. "I find it refreshing to be someplace where everything isn't hundreds of years old. Tell me, Miss Waterhouse, aside from the very formidable task of keeping an eye on your brother, how do you spend your days?"

She caught the jest, and smiled at him. Her eyes turned up just enough at the corners to give the impression that she was keeping a secret.

"Attending to Stuart's conscience is only one of many interests, Mr. Covington. I play the harp, and I work a great deal with Grace House, our local mission. It serves the city's many needy families. But you are correct—Stuart is my most pressing cause."

"I spend hours trying to outwit my sister, Covington." Stuart gave her a look that held both boundless annoyance and deep affection.

"All of San Francisco thanks you for your efforts, Georgia," replied another of the evening's dozen guests, Covington Enterprises' local manager, Dexter Oakman.

"And what would you say to this new fascination of ours, Covington?" asked Stuart. "Have you got any such heroes in Britain?"

"Pardon?"

"Robin Hood!" Oakman chimed in behind a mouthful of potatoes. "He's an English hero, isn't he?"

"Yes, he was," Matthew answered carefully. "The legend overshadows the real man, but often the best heroes are embellished, wouldn't you say?"

"Oh, no, Mr. Covington," Miss Waterhouse replied. "I quite disagree. The very finest heroes are the ones that aren't fictionalized."

"Fine, perhaps, but exceedingly rare," Matthew stated.

His hostess held an indefinable look in her eye as she murmured, "I would not argue with you there."

Stuart lifted his glass. "To heroes, then."

"Will we drink to all of them, or just this new fellow in your paper, Stuart?" inquired Oakman.

He rolled his eyes. "Drink to the Bandit if you must, but I'd much rather you drink to me."

"One must first do something heroic, Stuart," teased his sister.

He sighed dramatically. "To be so misunderstood."

"Is the fate of most great men," Matthew finished for him.

"Ah, Covington, I knew you'd come through for me. To our Bandit, then, and great—or should I say greatly misunderstood—heroes everywhere."

"And what do you think of our Bandit?" asked Mrs. Oakman, a round, rather witless-looking woman who had been engrossed in the minute dissection of her pork for most of the meal.

"Bandit, Mrs. Oakman?"

Stuart made a gesture as though he'd been stabbed through the heart. "I'm wounded, Mr. Covington. You don't read my paper?"

Well, that had been foolish. Thompson had truly seen to it that two copies came up to the room, but Matthew had fallen asleep over them, too exhausted to read the issue. And now Waterhouse knew. This trip was supposed to be Matthew's declaration that he could carry the family name with respect and reserve. He didn't need Georgia Waterhouse's fascinating eyes spurring him on to what his father called "his fantastic talent for making a spectacle of himself." Oh, the evening had taken a bad turn.

"Forgive me, Mr. Waterhouse. I pledge my loyal readership for the rest of my visit." It wasn't a very good recovery, but it would have to do.

Evidently not one to miss an opportunity, Stuart handed him a copy of the *Herald* the minute dinner had ended. Folded over to a back page, where some sort of serialized story had been printed.

Matthew read the first four paragraphs.

What?!

He quickly read them again, squelching the urge to gasp aloud.

Chapter Four

No.

Impossible.

Matthew sat down, hoping he showed no sign of the storm going off in his gut. He read the rest of the story, willing himself to look casual. Evidently the other night had been a spectacularly bad idea.

Don't jump to conclusions, he admonished himself. He knew who had witnessed the conflict in the alley that night, and none of them were reasonably able to document it. Several details were different.

Smile and leave it, Covington. Leave it alone. Leave it…

"Who is this George Towers?"

"Fine storyteller, isn't he? He's one of my, shall we say, hidden assets. The tale's been the talk of the town today. I hadn't been eager to run fiction in my paper until now, but I must admit I'm insanely pleased."

Talk of the town. Marvelous. Father would be so very… *intent on killing him.*

"I'd imagine you are." *Waterhouse had said fiction, hadn't he?*

"We haven't got a bumper crop of real heroes in San Francisco these days, so this author came to me with the idea of making one up. Seems to have hit a nerve. We may give your man Dickens a run for the money, eh?"

"Indeed..." That was all Matthew could spit out.

"I'll run one of these every week if the attention keeps up," Stuart announced.

"If I know you, Stuart," chimed in Dexter Oakman, "you'll run *two*."

Matthew made a mental note to never step out of his bedroom door after dinner *ever again*.

Which was ridiculous, wasn't it? Yes, the Bandit used a whip, and he wore dark clothes. And he had saved a child—granted, it was a small girl in this story, but in other details the story was alarmingly similar to what had happened.

Stop it. This was pure coincidence. It had nothing to do with Matthew. He had nothing whatsoever to do with bandits, black or otherwise.

He had just gotten his doubts under control when Georgia Waterhouse walked into the room.

"There's someone at the door to see you, Stuart. He's being rather insistent. Something about the presses."

She was slim and graceful. Her skin was the palest he'd ever seen, but it lacked the blue tint that lurked in so many of London's pale complexions. No, hers was infused with rose and gold.

Oh, Covington, his brain cautioned, *now's hardly the time.*

* * *

Stuart left the room barking instructions for Georgia to stay and seek Mr. Covington's opinion of his paper. The Englishman had the newspaper in quite a grip and for some reason she noticed his thumb was lying across the "George" of her byline.

"It seems my brother's not won the instant subscriber he was expecting, Mr. Covington."

"Pardon?" their guest swallowed.

"I gather you're not fond of the *Herald?*"

"Why would you say that?" he replied quickly.

"You're holding it as if it were a goose you planned to behead for supper."

It proved an effective metaphor. Covington made such a show of loosening his grasp on the paper that he nearly dropped it. Dexter Oakman laughed.

"Perhaps I should say I found it rather *gripping reading,*" Covington said wryly.

She smiled. "Stuart would like that."

The Englishman raised the paper again with a far gentler touch. "What is your opinion of your brother's venture into fiction, Miss Waterhouse?"

In all the hubbub about the story, Mr. Covington had been the first person to ask *her* opinion. And, perhaps most pleasing of all, he looked at though he really desired to know, and wasn't just making polite conversation. Perhaps it would not be such a difficult favor to keep him entertained, as Stuart had asked.

"It is one of the rare things Stuart and I agree on."

"I've no doubt," he murmured, in such a way as to make

Georgia wonder if he'd intended to say it aloud. There was something, a sort of puzzlement, coloring his words. He stared at her for the briefest of moments before shifting his attention to the fire. He had extraordinary eyes, Georgia thought. Dark blue, beyond indigo. As if God, forgetting that most dark-haired men had brown eyes, had given him blue eyes at birth, and then darkened the blue to cover the oversight. The inky blue-black of stormy waters. They strayed back to her for a moment, and she quickly looked away.

"Who is this George Towers? A local writer?"

"I know many things about the way my brother does business, Mr. Covington."

"But…"

"But I wouldn't be privy to half of them if I didn't know the value of a secret." Georgia allowed herself to hold his eyes for a moment. "Especially one that is becoming rather sought after." People wanted to know who George Towers was. The office had received numerous inquiries over the course of the day. Georgia was almost heady with pleasure at readers' response to her story. Having it be a secret only intensified the effect. She imagined she had looked like the cat that swallowed the canary all day.

Stuart burst back into the room. "All is well—or at least until the next disaster. Thank you, Peach." He gave her an affectionate peck on the cheek.

"You're welcome," she said, preparing to return to the ladies in the salon.

"Stay just a moment." Stuart took her hand. "I want you to hear what our guest thinks of the Black Bandit."

"I've yet to finish the story, Waterhouse," Covington protested. "You can't very well ask me to comment when I've read only a handful of paragraphs." He didn't much care for the article. Georgia could tell. And she knew in a heartbeat what Stuart was going to do next. Covington didn't stand a chance.

"Well, then, read the thing." Her brother smoothed out the crumpled paper and motioned to one of the high-backed chairs near the fire. "Better yet, read it aloud to all of us."

"Stuart..." Georgia began, thinking he was going a shade too far.

"No, really, Peach. The test of any good story is how it sounds aloud. Covington, you've a fine voice—that accent and all. Why don't you read it to us?"

"I..."

Stuart was having fun with her, Georgia knew. Giving her a chance to secretly enjoy her talent. It was a dreadful thing to do to a guest, especially one who clearly didn't relish the prospect, but she could help herself no more than Stuart could. The opportunity to sit and watch people listen to her words was far too enticing. She wanted to hear him read it. Very much.

"Please, Mr. Covington," she found herself saying. "Indulge us."

"Men who refuse Stuart Waterhouse live to regret it," teased Oakman, "generally in the next day's headlines!"

Covington knew he was cornered. Gathering his dignity, he sat down, took a deep breath and began to read the inaugural installment of the Black Bandit's adventures.

His voice flowed on, deep and musical. But there was an odd note in it, whether of shock or of fascination, she couldn't tell. And his whole body seemed to be reacting to the story, albeit subtly. His hands clenched the margins, and he shifted his weight two or three times. He stumbled on the paragraph that described the Black Bandit as tall and lithe, dark and powerful.

He put the issue down quickly as he finished, and Georgia thought, *Well, here's one reader not won over by the Black Bandit.*

Chapter Five

Desperate for the sleep that continued to evade him, and determined not to set foot outside and risk any association whatsoever with any bandits, real or imagined, Matthew settled for swinging his fencing foil around the hotel room as quietly as possible that night. He tried to block and parry as softly as he could, since he'd already roused Thompson once by knocking over a water pitcher. Even so, Matthew's final thrust skewered an item from the fruit basket on the sideboard.

He hoisted the fruit high, its weight making the foil wobble slightly as a sticky stream of juice began sliding down the blade.

Pathetic.

His San Francisco visit was not going well. And if he didn't sleep soon, he wasn't going to have a lick of business sense by the time he visited the shipping docks tomorrow. Matthew thought it a cruel irony that while he was forced to spend his day listening to the sleep-inducing rhetoric of

Dexter Oakman, the combination of a silly newspaper story and a stunning woman made nocturnal sleep impossible.

He stared at the pair of *Herald* issues that lay on the table, taunting him. They were staring back, ganging up on him, their dark headlines glaring unblinkingly. *No,* he thought, nearly declaring it out loud, *I will not read it again.*

It wasn't as if he needed to. He'd reread the piece enough times that he could practically recite it. Checking over and over for hints and similarities, for any sign that George Towers had been hiding in some dark corner of that alley. No, it was impossible.

Wasn't it?

Matthew took his handkerchief and wiped down the foil, licking sweet juice off one finger.

Georgia Waterhouse. What was it about her that intrigued him so? Some of it was obvious. Her relationship with her brother fascinated Matthew. He'd known sibling teasing from his younger brother, David, but there was far more competition than companionship between them. David was highly critical of Matthew, the principal heir. Entirely too eager, he suspected, to have the position for himself. David and his father seemed to agree on so much in life. Matthew had long felt that Covington Senior had never quite forgiven his wife for having their sons in the wrong order.

No, affection was a longtime stranger to the Covington household. In recent years the fighting had cooled to an impassionate, rigid tolerance.

Stuart and Georgia, on the other hand, had something unique, an obvious but indefinable bond. As if they knew a secret the rest of the world would never share. Matthew had seen such a look flash between his twin cousins. Something beyond language or gesture.

Then again, knowing Stuart Waterhouse's social and professional prowess, chances were those two *did* know a few secrets the world might clamor for. Hadn't she said she'd been "privy" to a few of Waterhouse's "hidden assets"?

A beautiful woman with big secrets. *Perfect.*

The downstairs clock chimed three. Georgia adjusted her pillow for the thousandth time. Sleep rarely eluded her, and she found this fit of wakefulness annoying. Try as she might, even with the help of her favorite psalms, her mind refused to quiet itself for the night.

Granted, it had been a splendid day. Spending hours watching people carry the *Herald* to and fro, listening to visitors at the newspaper office gossip and wonder about George Towers and his captivating Bandit.

"*My* captivating bandit," she declared to the curtain fringe, which offered soft, frilly nods in the breeze. She cast a sheepish glance heavenward. "Well, *ours.* Thank you, Father," she sighed, "for using Stuart and me in such a...satisfying way. Even if Stuart doesn't see it as such."

Georgia rolled over and elected to take stock of the evening. Entertaining wasn't really her gift, so perhaps analyzing the dinner and its guests might sufficiently bore her that she could sleep. She was a competent enough hostess—goodness knows Stuart invited people over constantly—but not the kind whose soirees made the papers. At least not without her brother's direct intervention. He usually whipped up a dramatic paragraph or two when the mood struck him, more for the titillation of his dinner guests than any further need to see his name in print. Georgia knew full well it was Stuart's power, and not her social prowess, that lured guests to the table. In truth, that suited her fine.

The Oakmans were dull but useful, present tonight because of their association with Covington Enterprises, Georgia guessed. No, it was clear Stuart had focused his attention on Matthew Covington. Aside from her brother's passion for all things English, Georgia guessed he'd sought out Covington—and asked that she do the same—for far more than his accent. The name Covington was familiar to businessmen in San Francisco. Their import holdings were considerable; Stuart told her that Covington Dry Goods kept half the finer stores in San Francisco stocked with European products. Stuart deemed them important enough that he made sure any Covington representative who came to town appeared at the Waterhouse table. The elder Covington had even been to dinner once, although a long time ago. Georgia didn't remember *him* looking like the man who'd come to dinner tonight.

What she'd noticed most about Matthew Covington was the extraordinary command he had of his body, which was athletic and graceful. Stuart galloped around a room, Oakman toddled, but Matthew Covington *strode.* It seemed an odd thing to notice—not like hair or eyes or a smile or such—but it struck her in a way she couldn't put a name to.

Georgia wondered how high those British eyebrows would go if he knew a *woman* had come up with the story of the Black Bandit. *And* penned it.

The clock chimed half past. No reasonable woman would

be up at three-thirty in the morning considering her publishing strategies.

Well, then, she thought as she reached for her wrap, *if Georgia Waterhouse oughtn't to be up, perhaps George Towers can be awake.*

She smiled as the opening sentence came to her. *Why not?* Dipping her pen, she began:

> "The Black Bandit finished cleaning his sword as the sun dawned over the mountains. Sleep had eluded him that night…."

"I had one hundred seventy-three reasons to decline your brother's invitation," Matthew said when he escorted Miss Waterhouse to an event a few days later.

Why he chose this to be the first thing out of his mouth when she entered the parlor, he couldn't say. He'd meant it as a compliment, but as the words escaped his lips he realized how insulting they could be.

Fine opener, Covington. Did you leave your manners in England?

Thankfully, she seemed to guess his intent—and his instant regret—for a small grin played across her face. Her response pleased him.

"Yet, at the moment," he continued in complete honesty, "I can't recall a single one of them."

"A clever save, Mr. Covington. Perhaps you might fare better if you told me why you said yes," she countered, adjusting the ribbon on her hat.

"First off, it's been made quite clear to me that one

takes one's life into one's own hands when declining Stuart Waterhouse."

"True."

"And secondly, you make infinitely better company than sums and inventories."

She scowled. "I'm afraid I don't find that much of a compliment. In my opinion, *most of the world* makes better company than sums and inventories."

"It depends on the sums," replied Matthew, holding the door open for her as they stepped out into the afternoon light, "and very little of *most of the world* could convince me to endure a musicale."

"Endure? But it's Gilbert and Sullivan. At Tivoli Gardens, no less. Stuart's favorite—and very British."

Matthew grimaced and offered her his elbow. "My point exactly. I don't like tea, either, you know."

She laughed. A lovely, bright laugh. "Well, there will be some of that, but I expect Stuart might be able to find you a cider. He'll be joining us a little while after the concert starts. Some paper emergency." She sighed. "There's *always* some paper emergency."

It was a grand spring day. Matthew felt the crisp bay breeze—and the delightful company—lift his spirits. Admit it or not, he'd been wondering how he could see her again. He'd have said yes if Stuart had asked him to escort Georgia to a quilting bee. "I expect your brother thrives on crises, doesn't he?"

"He seems to. Anything less would bore him."

"Stuart Waterhouse bored. It wouldn't be a pretty sight." Matthew gave a chuckle, thinking of how the man had sped around the room at the dinner party. How he seemed to everywhere at once, and hardly ever sat down.

Georgia suddenly stopped walking. She turned and looked up at Matthew with intensity, the sun playing across her hair and cheeks. "I spend a tremendous amount of time talking about Stuart, Mr. Covington." She lowered her eyes, as if her own comment caught her by surprise. "I…I should like it if that were not the case with you."

Matthew gazed at her, a sudden sympathy filling him. "I would like that very much." *Yes, very much.*

She broke the spell, picking up the pace again, a bit flustered. "I'm sorry. I don't know what made me say that."

"I do." It was Matthew who stopped this time. "You're much different than he. But people lump you together just the same. I've been lumped together with my father for ages, and we couldn't be more different. Yet everyone assumes I'm just like him. I have to admit I don't always enjoy the comparison."

"So you understand," she murmured quietly, but said no more.

Chapter Six

It seemed ages before the portly soprano and her equally portly tenor husband ended their first act. Matthew wondered how the usually fidgety Stuart could sit transfixed by such music, but he was clearly enjoying himself.

"Today's edition, Peach," he announced as he pulled a paper from under his arm at the intermission. "I'll go fetch us drinks."

Georgia folded the pages directly to the back cover. "Ah, here it is," she said. She began to read.

Before he could stop himself, Matthew leaned over her shoulder to peer at the headline: Returning by Demand: Another Episode of the Black Bandit's Adventures. He read on, drawn in despite himself.

> "The Black Bandit finished cleaning his sword as the sun dawned over the mountains. Sleep had eluded him that night, as it had many nights of late. The exertion of his battles, the welcome partnership of arm and

whip, the song of the sword as it sliced the night air—these things eased his spirits. But lately, even they had failed to give him rest."

Matthew blinked and stared.

Blinked again. Read and reread, his throat tightening.

It was all there. Again. As if George Towers had somehow crept inside his life. How could someone he'd never met put words to his thoughts with such wrenching eloquence? Towers seemed to understand the solace sought in exertion—but the two of them had never met. Sleep surely eluded many men, but how many understood the art of weaponry such as swords and whips? Who *was* this man?

Matthew turned away. *No,* the connections weren't there. The tension and the sleeplessness must have drawn his nerves too tight.

As he turned back, he saw that Georgia was still entranced by the story. He stared at her, sensing how completely opposite their reactions had been. Matthew wanted to put as much distance as he could between himself and that confounding piece of newsprint. She, on the other hand, looked as if she would crawl into the story if she could.

She must have sensed his stare, for she glanced up. Her eyes had a soft quality, as if she'd been someplace faraway and wonderful. Matthew tried to soften his own expression, but it was too late. She had seen his reaction—the fact registered on her face.

"You're not fond of the Bandit stories, are you, Mr. Covington?" Matthew swore there was disappointment in her voice.

"No, it's not that." He gulped almost instinctively, then groped for some reasonable explanation to give her, wanting to banish the gulf that had just stretched between them. "They're a bit...overwrought...for my taste."

"I see." Her words were cool and clipped.

"I'm sure there are many people who enjoy such tales," he stated, trying to salvage the conversation. But the damage had been done. Why did she seem to care so much about what he thought? Why did it bother him so to disappoint her? Matthew opened his mouth to say more, then shut it with a sigh, convinced that anything he added would only worsen the situation. *Well, Covington, you've botched that one thoroughly. Where's Stuart with those drinks?*

Georgia's hand tightened around the newsprint. She'd wanted him to like it. Which was nonsense, really. He hadn't enjoyed the first episode, so why should he suddenly relish the second? It was even more effusive than the first.

But she wanted him to like it. Her disappointment was as sharp as it was surprising. She drank her tea in silence while the men found something acutely businesslike to discuss.

She had been sorry when her brother sat between her and Matthew Covington before, but now was grateful to have Stuart between them for the second act. Yet, sure enough, Stuart pleaded yet another crisis once the applause ended, and asked Matthew to see her home. In his usual obliviousness to other people's feelings, her brother focused solely on his goal: ensuring that Georgia and Matthew saw a good deal of each other. She'd have to put a stop to that soon, favor or no favor.

They spent most of the walk home engaged in forced

bursts of small talk, grasping for the close atmosphere they'd enjoyed earlier. It seemed just beyond their reach. By the time they turned the final corner to her house, the gaps of silence grew uncomfortable.

Ten steps farther he stopped. He fiddled with his pockets some more, then looked up at her and said, "Would you…would you like me to read you the episode? You said you enjoyed it so much the other night at dinner. There's been so much rain, it seems a shame to go inside when the park looks so inviting." She watched him fumble, trying to cover his all-too-obvious desire to set things right between them. "I suppose we don't even need to discuss anything at all, just take in the view and…"

"Yes," she agreed eagerly. "I'd like that very much."

He smiled, a wonderful, warm smile. And when he pulled her hand into the crook of his elbow to cross the street, she felt the earlier glow come back.

He saw her seated on a wrought-iron bench under the shade of an enormous budding tree. He sat opposite her and made an amusing fuss of folding the paper to just the right spot. She sensed he was doing it purely to please her. What an appealing thing that was.

Clearing his throat so dramatically that it made her laugh, he began to read. Oh, gracious, his voice was wonderful when he read like that. Deep and refined, as if the words were both surprising and familiar at the same time. *How can he dislike the story and yet read it like that?*

"The night crept by, allowing him time to think of all he had done, and all he had lost. Justice seemed little comfort, and yet it was comfort enough. He could no more stand by and let evil run its course than he could quench his heartbeat."

Covington stopped reading and glanced up at her with an almost baffled expression. He seemed as if he didn't want to like her tale, but couldn't help himself. The words—*her* words—were affecting him; she knew it. He began to read again, and his voice seemed to wrap around her in the crisp air.

Matthew Covington was an exceedingly handsome man.

Mighty nice.

Stuart congratulated himself again for having the foresight to build the *Herald*'s offices so near his home. He hadn't realized until today what an advantageous view of the park the windows offered.

There was no mistaking the pair on the bench across from his front steps. Covington was reading the paper—his paper—to Georgia. And she was looking as if she enjoyed it immensely. Stuart smiled.

"Dex?"

"Yes, Stuart?" Dexter Oakman came up behind him, to stare out the windows.

"Will you look at that?"

"Seems your sister is playing hostess quite well. How'd you convince her to do it?"

Stuart turned. "My secret, Dex."

Oakman smirked. "You and your secrets."

"How far did Covington get in his audit this morning?"

"Halfway into last year's first quarter."

Stuart smiled with satisfaction. "I doubt it will be too difficult to see that he doesn't get much further than that."

"Sure looks like it."

Stuart brandished his file like a banner as he sang,

"I am the very model of a modern Major-General,
I've information vegetable, animal and mineral..."

Georgia set the paper down on the Grace House kitchen table and looked at Quinn. "Well, what do you think?"

The boy tore another large chunk of bread off the loaf she'd set in front of him before she began reading the original *Herald* installment aloud. He narrowed one eye as he pointed at her with the bread. "I *knew* somebody was watching." He grabbed his mug of juice with the other hand. "But a girl? Who's dumb enough to let a girl run the money home?" He took a gulp of milk large enough to make Georgia wonder if he was eating at all outside the meals she gave him at Grace House.

"That Bandit man'll be busy if things like this keep happening," Quinn said, raising his voice to be heard over the banging of pots and dishes in the mission's kitchen. He thunked his mug down on the rough wooden table where Georgia had set a place for him after he'd missed lunch by turning up late for the second day this week. Georgia winced a bit at the lavishness of her own home compared to the squalor she saw South of the Slot. The more she got to know Quinn, the more desperate his situation seemed. And there were so many more like him.

"Really," she said, still unable to find a way to convince

him the *Herald* wasn't reporting actual Bandit sightings. Quinn seemed to take such hope from the tale, she couldn't find it in herself to try any harder to take it away from him. Not that she hadn't attempted to. Quinn, it seemed, just wasn't interested in being convinced. She gave in to his insistent belief, half because she couldn't fight it, and half because she found she no longer wanted to.

"I hope Bandit Man gets to sleep during the day. If he's out all night, he needs to keep his strength up." The boy swiped his hunk of bread around the tin plate, picking up every last bit of food before he stuffed the bread in his mouth. "More egg?" he asked, his cheeks puffed out as he chewed.

Georgia rested her chin on her palm and raised an eyebrow at the grimy lad. He stared right back at her, until it apparently dawned on him what she was expecting.

"Fine." He grumbled, swallowed, then sat up straight. "May I please have another egg?" A more reluctant show of manners could not have been conceived. He made a face, as if the words left a bad taste in his mouth. The fact that he acquiesced to "please," "thank you" and napkins at all was further proof of how truly hungry he must have been.

Georgia smiled. "Most certainly. As a matter of fact, why don't we wrap up half a dozen so you can take them home." She leaned toward the boy as the house cook slid another egg—Quinn's third—onto his plate. "Does everyone have enough food at your house, Quinn?" While the answer seemed obvious, she wanted to hear his assessment of his own situation.

The lad looked at her as if she'd asked if the sky had recently fallen. "'Course not. Who does? I mean, 'cept for here." Somewhere in the background, Reverend Bauers's off-key baritone resounded as he worked. Georgia often felt God had never created a man more enthusiastic but less gifted in song. Still, San Francisco was a good place for him. The city's faults and vices could easily overtake a more sensitive soul.

"Da was yelling about being hungry just last night. Something about still not getting paid, but I think it was mostly his leg again. I sure hope he goes back to the docks soon. He's sour about having to sit around all the time."

A fight two weeks ago had injured Quinn's father's leg. The wharves seemed less safe with each passing week. Reverend Bauers had been patching up too many victims of dock fights recently. Georgia had to ask half her women friends to donate old shifts to be cut up into bandages. She'd even seen the reverend resort to whiskey to tend to wounds, because the medicinal alcohol was running low. Reverend Bauers had no musical talents, but he excelled at making do with what he had.

"I'm sorry to hear that, Quinn. I hope things will get better for you soon," she told him. "I'll see if Reverend Bauers can stop by and take another look at that leg." No matter how one viewed it, things seemed to be going from bad to worse in San Francisco lately. How long would Grace House be able to keep up with the load? What would happen when its small team buckled under the strain? *Heavenly Father,* she sighed, *stretch out Your mighty hand over this city. Things feel so desperate. What can be done?*

Georgia couldn't shake the sensation that God was answering when Quinn poked at the paper she was still holding.

"Miss Waterhouse, would you read it to me again? I like the part with the swords and all. I haven't seen his swords yet."

Again she felt the necessity of telling Quinn the stories were just made up by a man at Stuart's paper. And again, pity stopped her. If the Bandit kept one boy coming to Grace House, then the hero really *was* saving lives.

And Georgia Waterhouse could live with that paradox—at least for a little while.

Chapter Seven

"You can't be serious!" Matthew bellowed, trying not to let his splintered nerves get the best of him. One more sleepless night and he was going to become a threat to himself and others.

"I'm afraid I am, sir. I'm woefully sorry, but there it is."

"How? Exactly *how* did my whip go missing? It's not as if I leave the thing lying around, Thompson."

The valet, ever calm, seemed only mildly repentant—but then, the man's face was so professionally inexpressive that he could have been miserably guilty over the mishap and Matthew might never know. "It is hardly the type of thing to be left out in the open," Thompson said.

Matthew began overturning chair cushions. "Which is why I keep it locked up."

"Indeed, sir, you normally do."

He froze, cushion held midair, and glared at the old man. "'Normally'?"

"I must admit I was quite astounded to see it lying about.

Not having the combination to your arms case, I thought it best to at least put it out of sight. Under your linens, to be precise."

Matthew dropped the cushion back in place, heading for the bedroom, until logic stopped him. "But it's not there, is it?"

"I cannot see why the hotel staff would have thought to replace the linens twice in one day, sir. The bed had already been made. A mistake, I suppose. Change in chambermaids."

Matthew stood in the doorway between his bedroom and the sitting room, raking his fingers through his hair as he desperately analyzed the facts at hand. "So you put the whip in the sheets, and they took away the sheets, whip and all. Have I got it?"

Thompson folded his hands together, with just the mere hint of a wince. "I believe you do, sir."

What to do now? One couldn't go traipsing around a foreign city asking for a wayward whip. Matthew had visions of himself, crimson necked, trying to explain his odd choice of exercise to the hotel laundress. Then again, this was San Francisco. It might not prove to be the oddest thing she'd seen. He'd pay a discreet visit to the laundry, then, rather than have to deal with the hotel clerk or someone more likely to raise eyebrows.

Matthew pulled out his cuff links and offered them to Thompson. "I'll just have to go hunt it down, then, won't I?"

The valet looked at him askance. "Sir?"

Matthew dropped the links into the man's outstretched hand and started undoing his necktie. "I can't very well waltz into the hotel manager's office and demand my missing whip, can I? It's undoubtedly found its way to the laundry, and I'll just go fetch it back."

"Now?" As if to emphasize the lateness of the hour, Thompson produced his pocket watch and checked it.

"Better tonight than at breakfast tomorrow, don't you think? I can slip down to the laundries and slip back unseen if I'm careful."

In a rare show of disapproval, Thompson looked as if he found that a very bad idea.

Well, no, it wasn't a stellar plan, but Matthew had to get that whip back, and he wasn't swimming in good alternatives at the moment. "Have you a better solution, man?"

Thompson returned to a stone-faced silence.

"Very well, then. Don't wait up." Matthew rolled up his shirtsleeves in an attempt to look more common and less gossip worthy, should the laundry staff prove to have loose tongues. "And for goodness' sake, don't go hiding my belongings again, whatever you think may be the consequences."

Are you laughing, Father? Snickering in your velvet smoking jacket at the vision of your son, the indubitable Covington heir, sneaking toward the hotel laundry like some kind of cornered culprit?

Matthew's father had hated the whip from the moment his brother, Matthew's uncle, had given him the unusual weapon. "Ridiculous and overdramatic," Reginald Covington had declared with a frown when Matthew had showed him the first trick he had mastered. Here it was, the first accomplishment that was not just a mere shadow of his father's strengths, and it was dismissed with scorn. The whip was, and had continued to be, something entirely Matthew's own, which brought him a joy he couldn't ever quite put into words. Maturity had not yet changed that fact.

What a lark you'd have with my current pickle, Matthew thought, the familiar slant of his father's scowl coming to mind. *'Tis a good thing the Atlantic is as wide as it is.*

Why couldn't Thompson have misplaced the sword? It would prove so much less a problem, attract much less attention.

As he descended the third flight of stairs and caught the distinct scent of soapy water, Matthew thought of his valet's amazing ability to disappear. Somehow, Thompson could stand in the back of a room and evaporate into the wallpaper. One hardly even remembered he was there, until he would materialize—with a startling sense of timing—just when he was needed. The man anticipated needs with such uncanny skill that the rest of the household staff often declared he could read minds.

When Matthew was a young boy, the mere threat of Thompson's presence could stop him in his tracks. No matter how well Matthew hid his mischief, the man would always know.

Hesitating on the landing now, Matthew was struck by the irony that here he was, decades later, hiding mischievous deeds again. And Thompson still knew.

As he turned the last corner, the noise and scent told Matthew he'd found the laundry at last. He listened to the lilt of a woman's voice as she gossiped with someone over her work.

If he was careful, he could imitate their speech enough to hide his accent and, hopefully, his status. That had been a favorite trick of his youth—mimicking others' voices. It drove his father to distraction—which was, of course, its highest value. By the age of twelve Matthew could imitate relatives enough to fool even his sire momentarily. More than once Covington had threatened to ship his son off to the most vile form of punishment imaginable—the theater. Matthew knew, though, that the threats were hollow; the Covingtons would have endured anything before allowing an *actor* to taint the family name. Trouble was, young Matthew had more than once thought the stage might be a better life than one under his father's constant glare.

"Ain't it amazing what shows up in the laundry?" asked a gravelly old voice from the steamy room to his left. "Fine entertainment it is." A fowl stench hit Matthew as he inched closer to the open door. "Most of the time. Nicky, my boy, what is you boiling up back there? Smells like six-day-old fish!"

A man snickered. "You ain't so far off. Some old salt in one of the rooms done died, and nobody found him for two days. The manager got so mad he sent the entire staff back to change every bedsheet in the hotel all over again."

"I told you that man ain't got no more sense than I got eyesight," the old woman snarled.

"I ain't never fought you on that one, Neda. And him telling us to do somethin' so useless. Like it's our fault some girl missed a room, so's now we got to do double loads of wash to keep up."

The old woman grunted. Numerous piles of linens along the hallway confirmed that the laundry staff would be working through the night to catch up. Matthew poked his toe at one or two of the piles, hoping to detect the hilt of his whip among the soft folds. He wasn't so fortunate—the bedding billowed gently.

"If we're washing clean sheets all over again, then what's that awful smell?"

"The dead man's linens, Neda. Can you believe it? I said we should throw them out, but the manager says if we bleach 'em enough times they'll be good as new. Not me—you'd never catch me sleeping in sheets some old coot died in."

Matthew flattened himself against the wall and wrinkled his nose against the dreadful smell. Good thing no one had to come out into the hallway to do away with the questionable bundle.

"Well, whatever you think, take it outside, why don't you? I'm too old to be smellin' dead people's things, you sniggering fool."

"I *was* just hauling it outside, Neda. If you could see through those eyes of yours, you'd know that. Now stay where you are so you're out of my way whiles I go past."

So the laundress had bad eyesight. Matthew would never get another chance like this. He could be in and out with the whip—if she had it—by the time Nicky came back inside. Matthew let his head fall back against the wall. *I must be daft.* Reaching up, he mussed his hair and rolled his shirtsleeves higher.

"Hey," he said brightly, raising his voice in pitch and adopting the rusty Southern drawl he'd heard from the woman. "You all found a big black whip, by any chance? I'd heard it was down here."

"I told Nicky somebody'd come lookin' fer it." Neda was an enormous woman with dark, shiny skin and eyes that were a milky, unfocused gray. She sat precariously balanced on a small stool, surrounded by baskets of linens. A stack of perfectly folded facecloths rested in her lap. She swiveled her round head, with its knot of thick, braided hair, toward a shelf to Matthew's left. "That it?"

"Sure is," he said, wincing at his own comical effort to alter his voice.

"Well, fetch it on back to your master then, boy, 'fore Nicky decides to sell it, like he was plannin' to." She squinted at him, blinking repeatedly. "Big one, ain't you?"

Matthew grabbed the whip, keeping his eye on the door through which Nicky might return at any second. He hid his relief as his hand wrapped around the familiar hilt. "Huge, Mama says. Thanks!" he called as he ducked out the doorway, feeling as though he'd just gotten away with far more than he deserved.

He heard Neda chuckle loudly as he crept back down the hallway. "Hey Nicky, guess what? The Black Bandit just came and got his whip back. And you missed him. What do you think of that, Nicky boy?"

Chapter Eight

"That's servants' gossip." Georgia scowled. "Haven't you better sources than that?"

Stuart broke a flower off the hall arrangement—from the center again, as he always seemed to do, no matter how many times the house staff had asked him not to—and slipped it into his lapel. "Better sources than servants? They're the best sources there are, Peach. Now that our Bandit's a public mystery, everyone wants in on the fun. Of course, the promise of a few coins for Bandit stories doesn't hurt, either."

Georgia planted her hands on her hips. "You've wasted your money. Really, a whip loose in the hotel laundry? That's nonsense." She took a step closer to him. "Honestly, Stuart, isn't the Bandit selling enough of your papers? Now you pay people to invent collaborations?"

Stuart pouted. "You think so lowly of your own brother? Your own flesh and blood?"

"You are perfectly capable of such a thing."

He snatched his hat from the hands of the waiting butler. "Loath as I am to disappoint your high moral standards, this tale just happens to be genuine. A black whip showed up in the laundry at the Palace Hotel last night, and some tall young lad snatched it back before anyone could get a good look at it or at him. Absolutely Bandit-worthy, in my humble opinion, and straight from the mouth of a highly respected source."

Georgia frowned. "I've never known your opinion to be humble. Highly respected sources? In a hotel laundry?"

"On Mama's grave, Peach," Stuart said, leaning in and lowering his voice, "the whip's for real." He put on his gloves. "I wouldn't be surprised if it's the talk of dinner tonight at the Hawkinses. Mrs. Hawkins has become one of the Bandit's most ardent fans. Imagine that."

Georgia winced. Stuart knew his strategy. Bedillia Hawkins was by far the most excitable woman Georgia had ever met. If by some remote chance the newspaper account of a Black Bandit whip sighting didn't stir the public's imagination, Bedillia Hawkins would surely finish the job. It would be the town's juiciest gossip by sunrise. Stuart had probably made sure they would be dining at the Hawkinses tonight for just that reason.

"Don't you think, Georgia, dear?" Bedillia inquired of her obviously distracted dinner guest.

"Mrs. Hawkins?" Miss Waterhouse blinked, pulling herself back to the topic at hand. Matthew couldn't say he blamed her for her wandering thoughts. The conversation had been frightfully dull until the subject of the Bandit came up.

"I was saying, Georgia dear, how so much gossip seems

to be coming out of the Palace Hotel these days," repeated Mrs. Hawkins. "I was asking Mr. Covington if he finds it tiresome to be staying there, with so much going on. Bodies, thefts and whips—dear me, what will we see next?"

Matthew tried not to wince. He supposed he should be grateful they'd made it through the soup course before someone raised the dreaded subject.

The whip. Thompson's expression had been unbearable when he'd held out the *Herald*'s account of the wayward whip. There, next to the latest installment of the Black Bandit's adventures, was a tantalizing article about how a mysterious whip had surfaced in the laundry of the Palace Hotel. How a suspicious individual had stolen into the laundry and taken it back. Could the stealthy young man have been the Black Bandit himself? The text hinted at a variety of things that could set tongues and imaginations into motion all over the city. Based on Mrs. Hawkins's fascination with the subject, it had been successful.

"Do you think he's real, Miss Waterhouse? This bandit of your brother's invention?" Mrs. Hawkins winked at Stuart while she asked the question. It made Matthew wonder just how often people used Georgia to get to her brother. Judging from her expression, it happened frequently, and she found it highly irritating.

"The bandit or the author?" Miss Waterhouse nearly succeeded in hiding the edge in her voice.

"Why, the Bandit, of course. Everyone knows who the author is, even if they aren't saying." Mr. Hawkins raised his glass in Stuart's direction and let out a hearty laugh.

"Hawkins, you flatter me," Stuart said, lifting his glass in turn. Matthew noted he neither denied nor confirmed the insinuation.

Miss Waterhouse had to work to raise her voice above the resulting hubbub. "I find myself wishing he were real," she said, more sharply than he guessed she meant to. "I certainly would welcome him. San Francisco seems to be in dreadfully short supply of men with noble character—present company excepted, of course."

Matthew wondered, by the way she said it, if she'd added the last remark out of sheer obligation rather than any genuine respect for the men in the room.

"Georgia doubts my sources, Mrs. Hawkins. She feels I manufactured the whip's appearance to sell papers. That I'm printing shameless gossip rather than verifiable facts. As if I'd ever print anything but the honest truth."

"Stuart Waterhouse," laughed the rather besotted man next to him, "when have you ever printed the honest truth?"

"Miss Waterhouse, it seems to me that you endure much on your brother's behalf," Matthew offered, because it seemed that no one else in the room gave a thought to her obvious discomfort. "How do you find the strength?"

She smiled—just a bit, and only for a second, but it was a smile nonetheless. "Hours and hours of prayer, Mr. Covington. I have been known to take my frustrations out on the upper strings of my harp—I am forever breaking them—but mostly it requires endless prayer." She kept her tone light and conversational, but he noted an edge of weariness in her glance.

Matthew looked around the table and thought Miss Waterhouse must have a penchant for lost causes. "That's far too large a load for such delicate shoulders. Perhaps one ought to leave such a Herculean task to the likes of the Black Bandit." The last remark jumped out of his mouth seemingly of its own accord, before he had one second to think better of it.

"Speaking of Herculean tasks, Mr. Covington," declared Stuart, "I think it's high time you visited Georgia's precious Grace House. They're always working to save the world over there. What do you say to a tour tomorrow?"

"Appealing as it sounds, I am expecting some documents to arrive from Sacramento in the morning. Perhaps another time?"

Dexter Oakman nearly jumped out of his seat, opposite Stuart. "Oh, gracious, I'd completely forgotten, Covington. Meant to tell you before dinner." He put down his glass. "Those documents won't be in until Tuesday, perhaps Wednesday. The wire came in this afternoon."

"Well," said Stuart, smiling broadly, "events are conspiring in your favor, aren't they? Tour Grace House, then. Reverend Bauers and his high-minded companions will make excellent chaperones. I've even heard nuns work there."

"I hardly think Reverend Bauers has time to conduct social outings," said Georgia.

"Nonsense," her brother replied. "You might even convince Covington to send over a spot of money to help the needy." He turned to Matthew. "Mind your pockets, Covington. My sister can be most compelling when it comes to philanthropy."

Of that, Matthew had little doubt.

Chapter Nine

The clock chimed quarter past the hour as Stuart refilled his glass and Oakman's. "Did you have any trouble?"

Dexter winced. "Some. It took a bit more grease across the palm to get them diverted, but we'll see those ledgers from Sacramento before Covington does. We'll have to be careful."

Stuart picked up the poker and stirred the fire. The gold-orange flames flickered, reflecting in amber liquid in his glass. "I'm always careful. Georgia's just making my job that much easier. We practically waltzed into that tour of the mission this evening. I hadn't yet worked out how I was going to get Covington out of the office for a few hours in order to switch things. Honestly, I couldn't have planned it better myself."

"I did follow your line of thinking, Stuart." Oakman groaned, rubbing his leg. "Was it really necessary to bash my shin under the table? You've left a mark."

"Sorry about that, Dex." Stuart replaced the poker and walked over to the chair where he sat. "I hadn't time to be subtle. And speaking of marks..." He lowered his voice even though they were completely alone. "You're sure of this fellow? They'll be no trace of the alterations?"

Oakman drained his glass. "He's the top man, they tell me."

Stuart frowned. "Remind our friend that it won't go at all well for him if anyone can notice his...handiwork."

"Oh, I believe he knows." Oakman smiled.

"Make sure," Georgia's brother said, sipping from his own glass. "Show him your shin if you think that will help. I want no slips on this. Not one."

The man nodded, forcing a weak laugh. "Without a hitch, Stuart. It'll come off without a hitch."

Waterhouse began loosening the knot in his cravat. "Tell your wife there'll be a lovely piece about her dress tonight in the social column this week. She looked stunning at dinner, and we haven't run something about her yet this month. She deserves it."

"She'll be very pleased to hear that, Stuart. You're always so good to her. And Caroline does love to see her name in the columns, you know."

Everybody does, thought Stuart. *Everybody always does.*

"It's not a grand cathedral, but I rather fancy God enjoys it here." Georgia ran her hand across the adobe arch of the mission's side doorway, and a piece of the facade crumbled under her touch. "She's put up a grand fight over the years, and she's still standing. Reverend Bauers excels at what he calls 'making do at making do.'"

"That really means finding new sources for bandages, making food go three times as far, and squeezing yet one more use out of most any object," explained the reverend as he led Georgia and Mr. Covington out into the gardens.

They'd not gone three steps when a noisy commotion started somewhere off to their left, by the kitchens. Within seconds a pair of youths burst through the door, bundles in their hands. It was clear they hadn't expected to find anyone in the garden.

"Thief!" a voice cried from inside. "Stop them!"

Georgia gasped as she realized what the boys were carrying. Poking out of one of the bundles was a gold cross from the mission's tiny chapel. After glancing quickly at each other, they split up, running around the garden fountain toward the gate. Without any discussion whatsoever, Mr. Covington and Reverend Bauers set upon them, Covington taking the larger of the pair.

Georgia backed up to the fountain rim as a brawl broke out around her. "Help! In the garden!" she called as arms and legs thrashed.

As large as they'd seemed coming through the door, the boys were still rather young, and it was only a minute—albeit a dreadfully long one—before each was subdued. Grunting, they struggled against the grip of Reverend Bauers and Mr. Covington.

"How dare you!" the reverend huffed at his captive, as angry as Georgia had ever seen him.

In that second, the larger boy managed to pull out of Covington's grasp and slide something metal from his boot. It was a knife, which he quickly waved at Matthew.

No one moved. The mission cook burst through the door, only to freeze on the threshold as she saw the weapon in play.

Mr. Covington, however, somehow used that momentary distraction to grab a long stick from a pile behind him. He planted his legs in a defiant stance. How could he hope to defend himself with just a stick? *Oh, Lord, help him!*

Both combatants brandished their weapons, and it was instantly obvious that Mr. Covington knew exactly how to wield his, whereas the boy had evidently just grabbed a kitchen knife. Slowly, the man angled his body sideways, his rear arm high while he swung the stick through the air, coolly meeting each of the lad's angry thrusts.

The cook disappeared back through the door—going for help, Georgia hoped. She clutched the fountain rim, not caring if she soaked her sleeves, trying desperately to think of something she could do.

The smaller boy suddenly stomped on Reverend Bauers's foot, sending the two of them doubling over. Immediately, the larger boy lunged at Covington, who tossed aside his stick, trying to wrestle the knife from his opponent's hands. The lad only fought harder, slashing wildly at Covington's chest.

Lord Jesus, save him! Georgia nearly fell into the fountain, and a scream left her throat. The smaller boy took off through the gate with no thought for his conspirator. Reverend Bauers yelled for help as Covington struggled with the larger lad and his knife.

Georgia stood frozen and shocked. In all her time here, in all she had seen, no one had ever had the audacity to steal from Grace House.

Three men finally came rushing out the kitchen door, just as the blade sank into Covington's forearm. Georgia flinched at the sound of it ripping through the fabric of Mr. Covington's jacket. The Englishman gave a roar of pain, at which the wiry lad squirmed out of his grasp and leaped through the gate his companion had left swinging.

"We draw no blood in Grace House!" Bauers bellowed after him, rushing to Covington's aid.

Georgia was still clutching the fountain, unable to move as she watched scarlet ribbons creep out from between Mr. Covington's clenched fingers. He'd been stabbed. She'd seen Cook cut herself with a kitchen knife, but had never witnessed anyone being *purposely stabbed.* Her brain seemed unable to accept the concept.

"Georgia!" the reverend called. "Come here."

Covington's eyes locked onto hers. She tried to breathe, but it was as if her corset had tightened into a vise. Dimly, she saw him force a smile.

"Shall we go find me a bandage and dry you off?" he asked.

A thick, red drop of blood fell from his clenched hand and splattered on the flagstone, snapping her out of her stupor. She let go of the fountain, and the breath she'd been trying to take rushed suddenly into her lungs.

Reverend Bauers took off his coat and wrapped it around Georgia's shoulders. She really wasn't that wet, but she shivered as the clergyman slipped Mr. Covington's waistcoat off his good arm and bundled it around the injured one. "Since we've ruined your coat already, it might as well serve as a bandage until we get you inside. We might have to stitch you up, Covington. There are medical supplies in the next building—can you walk?"

Chapter Ten

A sharp scent made Georgia gasp. She felt the warmth of a hand on her shoulder.

"Miss Waterhouse?" a genteel voice was saying. It sounded foreign and yet somehow familiar. "Miss Waterhouse, can you hear me?"

"Hmm?" She rolled her head in that direction, waiting for the smoke all around her to clear. The sharp scent came to her again, making her cough.

"Georgia, my child," said a second voice, "wake up. You've been far too brave today. Open your eyes, child." A cold, wet cloth touched her brow, and she recognized the voice as Reverend Bauers's.

The sharp scent returned a third time, making her lurch forward and rasp in a breath. She grabbed the reverend's hand as the room spun around her.

"You fainted, Georgia," he said, with an affectionate laugh, "I told you to go home, and that there was no reason to sit through my stitching Covington up. You are more stubborn than that brother of yours at times."

With a white-hot flash that made her eyes open wide, Georgia recalled her circumstances. How foolish she had been to insist on staying through the gruesome task. "Dear me. I'm so dreadfully sorry to have caused such a fuss."

"It's I who should be offering the apology," said Mr. Covington, looking much better than the last time she remembered seeing his face. "This was no place for a lady. Even a very brave lady." He held up a bandaged arm. "You'll see I've made a fine recovery, and I should never forgive myself if you do anything less than the same." He leaned in, his dark brows furrowing in concern. "Are you quite all right, Miss Waterhouse?"

Georgia blinked and took a deep breath, then dabbed at her face with the cool cloth the reverend offered. "Yes. Yes, I think so. Although I'd find a glass of water very welcome."

"Stay off your feet, Covington," said the reverend, pushing himself up from the floor, where he knelt in front of Georgia. "I'll go fetch our brave Miss Waterhouse a glass of water, and perhaps a bit of apple for the both of you. It's been a trying morning, wouldn't you say?"

"Most trying, indeed," she said, fussing with the reverend's coat, which was still wrapped around her. She really wasn't as soaked as everyone seemed to believe. "I'm afraid I've proved a miserable guide, Mr. Covington."

"Not at all," he replied. "I can't remember the last time I've had such a lovely lady swoon on my account." A wide, warm smile flashed across his face. "It's done marvels for my spirits." He nodded toward his bandage when Georgia blushed. "And the arm should heal quickly." He returned his gaze to her face and let it linger for a moment.

Georgia felt the room begin to spin again. "Gracious, I don't believe I've ever seen a larger needle." She fanned herself with the cloth and sat up a bit straighter.

Covington cast a glance toward the table, still cluttered with the bloody tools of his treatment. "I must admit, I have seen smaller, and I'll confess to an unkind thought or two toward the beastly thing in the last hour." He turned to face her again, and she noticed that his hair was in disarray, spilling wildly over his forehead. He had such dark, glossy hair for one with eyes of blue.

"But I *am fine,* Miss Waterhouse, and I have no doubts whatsoever about my full recovery." He fumbled with his shirt collar, struggling to raise his injured arm high enough to fasten the button. "I'll be summing up ledgers by the day's end, I'm afraid."

Georgia reached out to help him, then stopped herself. Red-faced, they both retreated, suddenly aware of their inappropriate proximity. Even under the unusual circumstances, they were sitting entirely too close. Mr. Covington cleared his throat and used his good arm to draw his chair toward the table.

It seemed an eternity before the reverend returned. He offered a small cup to Georgia. "Here's water for you now, but I think it's best we have something to eat in the dining room and let them clean up here. Take my arm, Miss Waterhouse, and mind you walk slowly."

When they were seated in the mission's meager dining room, Reverend Bauers produced a small packet, which he placed on the table. "I regret your visit wasn't a pleasant one, Covington. So I'd like to give you this. It comes with a bit of a story that I think you'll appreciate, given the circumstances."

"There's no need," the Englishman argued.

Reverend Bauers huffed and pushed the packet toward Georgia. "Open it for him, will you, child? I'd just as soon that wounded arm stayed resting on the table, Covington."

Georgia opened the wrinkled brown paper—on its sixth or seventh use, she mused—to reveal a small Bible. It was old and well used, and had a chunk missing from the middle, as if someone had carved a bite out of it, like a steak. The pages had been cut clean through to somewhere in the Psalms.

"Seen a bit of wear, this Bible has," said the reverend.

Georgia handed the small, leather-bound book across the table to Mr. Covington, who held it up and squinted at the cover. "Looks as though someone took a knife to this," he remarked.

Reverend Bauers chuckled. "As a matter of fact, that's exactly what happened. I wore that Bible in my breast pocket throughout my travels in the islands. I served our Lord setting up no fewer than four churches in Hawaii. We did not always get the warmest of greetings." He pointed to the gap. "A spear thrown at my heart took out that bit. Saved my life, it did."

He motioned for Georgia to search the coat she was wearing, and sure enough, in the breast pocket she found a small Bible nearly identical to the one Mr. Covington was holding. Only this one had a black leather binding and was still intact.

"I've taken to always wearing one over my heart. And I've been looking to pass this on to the right man ever since." The reverend paused and gazed at his guest. "I think it ought to be you, Covington."

"I can't accept this. It saved your life."

"You saved Grace House from theft, my son. And came

out much worse for your effort. No, no, I'll not be refused. You must have this, I insist."

Covington looked at Georgia. "I implore you, Miss Waterhouse, reason with him. It's far too dear a gift. I simply can't accept it." He slid the Bible across the table toward her.

She put out her hand to stopped him. "I would think it's become all too clear to you by now that Reverend Bauers cannot be refused. Accept the gift with gratitude, Mr. Covington. After all, as the reverend is all too fond of saying, God is on his side." As she spoke, Georgia felt something very close to a wink—the sort of playful glance she would give Stuart over the head of a dull dinner guest—spark in her eyes. It lasted a fraction of a second—a heartbeat, really—but seemed to stretch on in time. Their hands lingered on either end of the Holy Book, and she had the sensation of something important transpiring. It was nothing she could name or even really recognize; rather, the sort of flash one would put down to an overactive imagination or insufficient sleep. A "hunch," Stuart would have called it.

But he would have been wrong. It was something else entirely.

Reverend Bauers might have called it "the wind of the Spirit," but that would not be entirely correct, either.

Georgia spent the entire carriage ride home, and the ensuing afternoon sequestered in her rooms, trying to put a name to it.

Some part of her already knew.

Chapter Eleven

Stuart, how could you?

Georgia roamed through the house, fuming. For a moment she stopped in the dining room, but she had no taste for breakfast. Clutching the offending newspaper, she headed toward the parlor.

I cannot believe you've done this!

She pushed through the enormous double doors and stood in the center of the opulent room. It seemed stifling. Even though she'd chosen many of the furnishings, because Stuart had no patience for such things, she could see none of her own touches. Stuart's character was all over the house. He was everywhere, and Georgia seemed invisible. Frowning, she spun on her heels, heading toward his study.

He'd done the unthinkable. Betrayed their agreement in the worst way. She simply stood in the doorway, betrayal choking down all the words she wanted to say.

"Oh," he said after what seemed like hours, finally noticing her presence. How could he look up from his papers like that, as if she'd just breezed into the room to ask about the weather? "So you've seen it?" His voice was casual, almost dismissive. It incensed her.

She dropped the paper onto his desk, astounded that he—her own brother—couldn't see the pain he'd caused her. "How could you?" she finally asked, sounding so weak she wanted to kick herself.

He sighed, more in frustration than sympathy. "I own the paper, Peach. And I edit *all* my writers. Why should you be any different?"

It stung beyond her ability to describe. He would never see the enormity of what he had done. Why had she expected to be exempt from Stuart's legendary meddling?

"Because I *am* different," she retorted, wishing she had a more clever argument. "You added to my story. Something silly that shouldn't ever have been in there."

"*Embellished.* I embellished. It needed something to lighten up all that drama. Really. Carrying a Bible over his heart? With a knife mark in it? It was too much. You should be glad I didn't cut that part out altogether. I had to give the readers something a little more real. And you hadn't given him a calling card yet."

"A what?"

"A calling card. A sign that the Black Bandit had been there. It's in every good story, like a signature. Terribly dramatic. People will love it."

"A white ribbon nailed to a tree?" In Stuart's version, the Bandit had left a white ribbon nailed to the tree above the villain's head. Georgia found it ridiculous. As if her mysterious hero was wandering the streets of San Francisco with ribbon and tacks in his pocket like a hatmaker.

"Well, black seemed too morbid. It's a delicious irony, the Black Bandit leaving a white ribbon. I thought you'd appreciate that."

She appreciated nothing of the sort. "You could have asked." Georgia had taken this astounding risk, reached for this impossible dream, and he'd run over her. Like he ran over everyone. *Lord, how could You let this happen? I was so certain this came from You. And now...*

"Trust me. It'll run like wildfire." His condescending tone sliced at her—not because he was being deliberately cruel, but because he truly had no idea how much he'd hurt her. "You'll see," he said, returning his eyes to his work. "I'm very good at what I do."

Yes, Stuart, you're very good at what you do. She stood planted in the doorway, paralyzed with frustration at not being able to tell him how she really felt.

But would that change anything? Stuart would not suddenly soften his tactics because she had been the target this time. The paper was out. The calling card had been added. Her hero had been tainted by her brother's never-ending exploitation of everything he touched. Why had she expected better of him?

"You could have asked me to add a calling card of my own design," she said after a long pause, disgusted with the weakness of her voice.

"I don't ask," Stuart declared, obviously finding her suggestion ridiculous. "Not anyone. Not even you."

Matthew stared at the six columns before him, absent-mindedly feeling for the bandage knotted under his shirt-sleeve. He kept seeing the face of Georgia Waterhouse, her pale lashes resting against alabaster cheeks, her head tilted against the sturdy back of the chair, her creamy fist still clenched around the handkerchief. It was absurd that he found her so stunning in a dead faint. One does not, after all, look one's best when keeling over. She had "fainted in his best interest," as he'd put it when he recounted the entire morning's events to an astounded Thompson—yes, visibly astounded, and that was worth something! The whole incident endeared Miss Waterhouse to him.

Matthew did omit one detail to Thompson. He found he did not want to speak of the small, battle-sliced Bible that the reverend had handed him with such unsettling reverence. At first, Matthew thought his reluctance to accept the token was born of the clergyman's great affection for it—he'd not merited so dear a gift from someone he'd just met. As he carried it home, he realized that the reluctance came from the feeling that he was standing on a very slippery slope. Had things not come to such dire ends with the whip, Matthew confessed he more than once thought to hide the Bible under his blankets.

When he opened the morning paper, he wished he had.

Chapter Twelve

There it was in the newest episode of the hero's adventures: the Black Bandit and his own battle-scarred Bible. It could only mean Stuart Waterhouse was writing the Bandit stories himself. Given what Matthew knew of him, it was easy to believe Waterhouse penned his paper's greatest sensation. Georgia must have told him the story of the Bible, and he'd used it in the Bandit's adventures. A foolish act, as it gave away his identity.

Or did it? Perhaps Stuart wasn't as foolhardy as he seemed. Only three people in the world knew the source of the tale, and none of them had any interest in angering Stuart Waterhouse.

"Mr. Covington, sir?" A bright-faced clerk rapped on his office door. Matthew set down his pen and looked up from the ledgers. "There's a Reverend Bauers here to see you."

So someone else has been surprised by the morning paper, Matthew thought as he stood up and pulled off the black sleeves that protected his shirt from the ledger ink. He harbored a moment's ingratitude toward the reverend as the sleeve bumped painfully over his wound. Crude as the stitches were, he found he couldn't bring himself to have the wound redone by another surgeon. Not only would it be embarrassing to have to recount how one small street urchin had bested him in a fight and skewered his arm, but Matthew was certain the reverend would be coming to check on his "patient," and would feel disappointed that he had chosen to seek care elsewhere. Matthew's father was always boasting about the ghastly war scar on his left shoulder, and now Matthew had a ghastly scar of his own to boast about. As to its source, well, perhaps he'd omit some of the less heroic details when he told his father.

"Covington," Bauers called as he bustled into the room. He carried, not surprisingly, a copy of the *Herald,* as well as a small bag Matthew was sure presaged further medical atrocities yet to be endured. "How are you, my son?" The reverend pointed to his arm. "Healing well?"

"I had all but put the incident behind me," Matthew lied. "That is, until I read the morning paper. Seems we share a bit of the Black Bandit legend now, don't we? Do sit down." He came around his desk and motioned for the reverend to take one of the high-backed chairs that faced his desk.

"I suspected Mr. Waterhouse all along," Reverend Bauers said in a hushed voice as he eased his considerable frame into the chair. "Now we can be certain, can't we?" By his expression, Bauers enjoyed his newfound secret celebrity. "I must say I never thought I'd see the day when Stuart Waterhouse wrote about the Bible. God is full of splendid surprises." He chuckled, patting the folded paper on his lap.

"Will you reveal him?" Matthew asked, welcoming any topic that kept Reverend Bauers from opening that bag. Diversionary, yes, but he was curious to know what the reverend planned to do regarding Stuart. Several of the "men of God" Matthew had encountered back in England wouldn't hesitate to parlay such a secret into several sizable contributions if they found themselves in the clergyman's position. Everyone knew George Towers didn't really exist, but part of the Black Bandit story's attraction was its mysterious author. Stuart knew the mystery helped line his pockets, and he probably would consent to a few "acts of charity" to preserve it. Still, Matthew doubted the reverend would be the kind of man to pursue extortion, even for the sake of his ragged little flock.

"Oh, I suppose there's some that would try to use it for their own gain," Bauers replied, echoing Matthew's thoughts. "I'm sure if I went to see Mr. Waterhouse, I would come away with several tidy gifts. I confess I thought of it, for an instant, last night when yet another chair broke in the dining room. I find myself having great fun with the secret of it all, however. And if it means Stuart Waterhouse will actually have to pen the word *Bible* a few more times, then I am all for letting him run with our tale." The clergyman leaned close. "Ah, but Mr. Covington, could you not expose him as easily as I? After all, you've got the Bible now. I do wonder what the good Lord has in the offing with this one."

Matthew had not yet considered the idea of God somehow placing this particular Bible in his particular hands. It was an odd, squeamish thought to entertain. "What do you make of the Waterhouse family, Reverend? Did you know Georgia and Stuart's parents at all?"

Bauers either took the bait or chose not to recognize the diversion. "Alex and Audrey Waterhouse? No, but one hears things. I know Alex was the one to move the family business away from shipping into a variety of other interests, not the least of which is the newspaper Stuart now runs. Mrs. Waterhouse, from what I've been told, was a very great woman. Much like Georgia, I think. Very strong faith and a good, strong spirit. I'm not at all sure what she'd think of Stuart these days."

Matthew eased back in his chair and leaned his weight on his good hand. "And what do people think of Stuart Waterhouse these days?"

Reverend Bauers paused, stroking his chin. "He can be a very great friend. Or a greater enemy. Still," said the reverend, opening his bag, to Matthew's growing distress, "I wonder if Stuart has even an inkling of all the good he's doing."

"Whatever do you mean?" inquired Matthew, half out of curiosity and half to keep the man's hands out of that blasted bag.

"Oh, I know Stuart Waterhouse only thinks he's landed on a new way to sell papers, but God is no stranger to using bad intentions for good. Take the book of Genesis, for example. Joseph's brothers hardly had good intentions when they sold their little brother into slavery. God took their evil plot and used it to save thousands of lives." Reverend Bauers held the paper up. "If Stuart could see what I see, how people believe the tales to be true because they *need* the Bandit to be real, it would frighten him to bits. Georgia is proud of her brother, despite his motives, because he gave San Francisco what it needed most—a hero. I'd like to think you wouldn't be sporting that—" he pointed to Matthew's wound—"if our young friend had had a better start in life and more men of character to show him how to behave."

"Did you catch the thieving little urchin?"

"We did. And he was punished. Not to defend him, but you might steal as well if your father had poured all his wages into the bottom of a glass and your family hadn't eaten in three days."

Matthew fingered the knot on his bandage again. "Hard times are no excuse for criminal behavior."

"Oh, he's a bad seed, I'll grant you that. But all these boys know is cheating. Dockworkers are cheated out of fair pay as often as you and I breathe. If there's no justice around, you quickly learn to take all you can just to live. Steal to eat. Lads learn by example." The clergyman heaved a sigh and set about opening the bag again.

"Surely men of the cloth such as yourself can show them a better course," Matthew said, attempting to keep the conversation open and the bag shut.

"Come now, Mr. Covington!" The reverend spread his pudgy arms wide. "Do I look like the focus of a young man's aspirations? I've no curves to capture their hearts and no gallantry to capture their minds. Oh, no, Covington. Surely you can see why Miss Waterhouse thinks the Bandit is such a fine idea. A swashbuckling man of mystery is just the thing to turn these young imaginations around. The Black Bandit may be the best thing Stuart Waterhouse has ever done for us." Bauers chuckled as he pulled at the drawstring of the small brown bag. "Unless, of course, our Mr. Waterhouse can make his Bandit come to life. Now that'd be nothing short of a wonder."

He produced some wicked-looking scissors and a bottle of something Matthew was sure would result in considerable pain. "Now, Covington, let's see to that arm."

His arm had been stinging for hours. That was his excuse. Surely the pain had driven him to such foolishness.

The pain and the harrowing tales he had heard that afternoon.

After Bauers had left, Matthew's arm stung so badly he decided further ciphers would be out of the question. He shifted his attention to the shipping interests of Covington Enterprises. A couple of inquiries had led him to a contact, a clerk within the offices who dealt repeatedly with dockworkers and marine merchants.

Matthew didn't like what he found.

An hour or two with the clerk not only confirmed Reverend Bauers's dire assessments, it exceeded them. Commerce on the docks, if one could even stretch to call it such, was nothing short of piracy. London's worst corners held more justice than San Francisco's docks. So far Covington Enterprises appeared innocent of such behavior, but given such a culture, Matthew couldn't be certain. It was standard practice to promise immigrant workers one wage and then pay another after a long day's labor. One company's shipments moved swiftly through the docks while another's rotted in plain sight.

Matthew had heard enough to sour his stomach.

And that's why he'd done it.

Well, that and the fact that he couldn't sleep. A man's mind plays tricks with his good sense at three in the morning.

He hadn't set out to head South of the Slot at that hour—no man in his right mind would consider such a thing. He hadn't set out to do anything. It just overtook him, like a wave sweeping out to sea.

And somehow, with no forethought, as if someone else had moved within his own body and the way had been cleared for him, the deed was done.

He came back near dawn, exhausted, and astonished at his own actions. Thompson asked where he had been, but he didn't answer. Thompson stared at his exposed wound and asked if he wanted a new bandage, but Matthew still said nothing.

Mostly because he had absolutely no idea what to say.

Chapter Thirteen

"Quinn? How on earth did you find your way here?"

"You have to come, now. Reverend says so." The boy looked pressed for time, but not upset. What could bring him here this early in the morning?

"Is everything all right? Is the reverend ill?"

"No, ma'am. He's jumping around like it's Christmas." Quinn stared past her to the breakfast table visible through the dining room doors. "He sent me to get you right away. You have to come now, Miss Georgia." The boy looked past her skirts again, licking his lips. "I think he'll explode if you don't."

Georgia watched the lad's sense of urgency war with the scent of bacon wafting out from behind her. "Quinn, has no one offered you a bit of breakfast for your efforts?" she inquired, trying hard to keep the laughter from her voice.

"No, ma'am!" His eyes widened in hungry hope.

"Well, I'm all for rushing to Reverend Bauers's aid, but I have a few things to attend to that will only take a moment.

Why don't you busy yourself with a plate in the kitchen while you wait. I won't be but a..."

Before she had even finished, Quinn was bounding down the hallway.

A small crowd circled Grace House, when Georgia and Quinn arrived in her coach. Several families stood in the courtyard with Reverend Bauers, chattering excitedly. Some great news had obviously reached the mission. If he already knew, Quinn's mouth was sealed; he claimed he'd been told to be silent.

It took a few moments to find it. After all, one would have expected something far larger, given the commotion. Eventually, after a question or two, she was directed to something small on the Grace House doorpost.

At which point Georgia nearly stumbled.

Money.

A good deal of money, from the looks of it.

Nailed to the doorpost with a white ribbon.

The world grew still for a moment, as if startled into silence by the sight. Her gaze swayed to Reverend Bauers, who met her eyes with an expression of astonishment that surely matched her own.

Nailed to the door with a white ribbon.

Then, suddenly, she caught sight of more white ribbons. Dozens of people clutched a white ribbon and an actual dollar bill. It may have been the first time any of them saw or held, much less possessed, paper money. A dollar was no small amount, but a *paper* dollar—that was a double surprise.

God, in His infinite wisdom and humor, had taken Stuart's ugly twist and turned it into something splendid.

"See?" spouted Quinn. "The Bandit!" Georgia marveled that the child had been able to keep quiet at all, given the sparkle in his eyes as he pulled her forward.

"Can you believe it?" Reverend Bauers was beet-red from the excitement. "Have you ever in all your years…" He couldn't finish the sentence.

Georgia could only shake her head. She was afraid to speak, sure she would give herself away if she uttered even one syllable.

The money had been nailed to the top of the archway, about nine feet off the ground. The white ribbon fluttered in the breeze, and hands from the crowd reached up to touch it, as though it would bless them on contact. When she'd read Stuart's passage, Georgia had envisioned a frilly white ribbon—something off a hat or dress. This was a simple strip of white cloth—not fussy, but noble and absolutely perfect.

"Come, lad," Reverend Bauers called, pointing to Quinn. "What do you say we get this down and put it to good use?"

The boy sprinted toward the reverend, who hoisted him up to reach the nail. It did not come free easily, and in the end three men had to hold Quinn up while he wiggled it loose. When he finally succeeded, and was lowered into the crowd clutching the money and the ribbon, a cheer rose up. Georgia absorbed every detail so that she could tell Stuart. Even he couldn't remain unaffected by the scene unfolding before her.

Hope had come South of the Slot.

God had brought it. Invited by the persona of her Black Bandit.

Her satisfaction was so deep, so complete, that if the world never knew of her role, it would be more than fine.

Thank You, Lord, Georgia prayed as she watched Reverend Bauers lock the money up in the mission safe a few minutes later. Fifty dollars would go a very long way in his resourceful hands. *Thank You so very much for giving me such a laughable idea and turning it into this. I'm blessed beyond words.*

The reverend dusted off his hands and turned to her, grinning from ear to ear. "I never thought I'd have occasion to say this, child, but God bless Stuart Waterhouse."

"Stuart?"

"Come now," said the clergyman, pulling her a bit closer while he lowered his voice. "Do you think I don't know? It's obvious the Bandit is Stuart's doing, so don't try to hide it." He narrowed one eye playfully. "Although I'd mind what you say around him from now on. After this hits his presses, he's liable to pounce on any story you tell him. It's a good thing Mr. Covington seems sporting about the whole matter, I'll tell you that."

So they all thought Stuart wrote the Bandit stories.

Well, of course they did—it would be the natural conclusion of anyone who really sat down to think about it. And surely now the reverend and Mr. Covington had every reason to think Stuart was George Towers. They'd naturally assume she'd told Stuart the story of the Bible, and he'd used it. Such behavior was expected of him.

But Stuart hadn't done it, had he? No, she had. She had done something so "Stuartlike" that everyone immediately attributed it to him. Not a compliment to her character.

Still, look what God had accomplished with it. Did that mean she had done the right thing? Or that God had made good come from her poor choice? The fact that there was no clear answer was disturbing indeed.

"Why yes, of course, that's quite right," she said, trying to hide her tangle of emotions. The few minutes she'd had were simply not enough to digest today's wild turn of events. Georgia felt as if her head and heart were turning somersaults in twelve directions.

"It's a fine, fine day." Reverend Bauers beamed. "Just last night I was beseeching our Lord to send help for the back staircase. I was hoping we'd get another year out of the floorboards, but..." He shook his head, the tops of his ears turning pink as he chuckled yet again. "Fifty dollars. Glory be to God! Fifty dollars."

"It is an amazing thing," Georgia said, meaning every word.

"And long overdue in coming, my child." Reverend Bauers fiddled with the white ribbon someone had tucked into his coat pocket. He looked up, a thoughtful expression on his chubby features. "You must tell Mr. Covington at once. He will be delighted, I think, after having seen the worst of our little flock."

Georgia smiled, thinking how grand it would be to watch news of this fly through the city. "Stuart has invited him to dinner tomorrow, so I shall make sure he hears of our little wonder. It is a good day, Reverend," she said. "Go and enjoy it."

Chapter Fourteen

Georgia found Stuart standing over the printing presses. There on the stairway above the rows of black, greasy machines, he was king of all he surveyed. The day's edition had been rerun with a detailed account of what Stuart called "The Generosity at Grace House."

"Look at them, Peach." He spread his hands, gesturing to the roaring machines. "Whirring away. It's just ink and paper, but it's so much *more* than ink and paper." He burst into a chorus from *The Gondoliers.* "Did I not say it would be spectacular? I've even ordered white ribbons for the floral arrangements at dinner tonight." He stopped swaggering and crossed his arms in thought for a moment. "I may even have them string up the trees on the front walkway. Ribbons everywhere. What do you think of that?"

That was Stuart—excessive in every detail. "I think it rather much," she replied. Then again, "rather much" was what people expected of her brother. "There will be no white ribbons in my hair tonight, so don't even think of asking."

The look on his face told her she'd accurately predicted the limits—or lack of limits—of his excess. He was, obviously, planning to ask her just that. She shook her head, but couldn't help smiling at his rampant happiness. His pleasure meant something to her, because he was the only person who knew the Bandit's true source. Even if he had twisted it beyond her liking, the partnership had been fruitful beyond her bravest dreams.

At that moment, despite his faults—and the faults he seemed to drive her to—she loved her brother.

Matthew made the coachman go around the block again when he pulled up to the Waterhouse mansion. The sight ruffled him so much he needed several minutes to summon his composure.

Not that the Waterhouse mansion wasn't an impressive sight on its own, having the unmistakable appearance of an owner who didn't know when enough was enough. But tonight, it looked like a frosted cake. The ornate house and grounds were literally covered with white ribbons.

I suppose I deserve this, Matthew chided himself as they rounded the corner to see the ribbon-bedecked house for the second time. His stomach seemed to sink to the soles of his boots as they started up the inclined drive. *It always ends up in something like this, and you never learn. Never.* Matthew slumped down in his seat, wishing he could somehow render himself invisible.

But wait, you are. No one knows you were the one. Surely, if people knew, they'd have been on you like bees on honey by now. You're safe. He pulled in a breath and straightened his collar.

Just don't ruin it.

Had the invitation come from anyone but the Waterhouses, Matthew would have made his excuses and kept to his room. Even if it meant an entire evening of ignoring Thompson's suspicious glare. And the valet did suspect something. After a lifetime of Matthew's antics, the man had frighteningly good instincts about what Matthew did or didn't do out of his sight. But even Thompson, for all he might suspect, would never reveal anything.

It was worth any discomfort, Matthew decided, to see Miss Waterhouse's reaction to his little stunt. The whole time he'd been darting in and out of shadows, shredding his bandage and inventing ways to hammer silently, his mind had played with the image of her face. How she would react. How those porcelain cheeks would flush with joy at the sight of those ribbons fluttering in the breeze.

He'd done it for her. He told himself over and over that he hadn't, but the truth refused to subside. Her high expectations for mankind had tugged something out of him. So he'd done it. He'd gone out and made that fictional hero display some of the philanthropy she so valued.

It felt marvelous, reckless, and he'd never slept better.

Good thing, too, Matthew thought as he pulled himself out of the coach and cringed at the cascade of white ribbons dripping all over the house. *You'll need every wit you have about you tonight.*

Stuart Waterhouse looked as though he'd been crowned king of California. Within ten seconds of saying hello,

Matthew was dead certain Stuart was the pen behind the Black Bandit. He was strutting like a peacock, cleverly dodging the constant questions about the Bandit's white-ribboned generosity. For a man who loved intrigue and sensation, today must have felt like a thousand Christmases wrapped into one.

Even with all the other secrets abounding that night, Matthew was keenly aware of the one secret he shared with Georgia Waterhouse: that he owned the Bible of Black Bandit fame. Bauers knew, and probably Stuart knew, as well, but that didn't alter Matthew's feelings.

She knew. It played across her face whenever her gaze flickered his way, driving him daft for most of the evening until sometime after coffees were poured, when Matthew managed a word with her in a corner of the library.

"My dear Miss Waterhouse," he said, astounded at his sudden craving to say her first name despite the social outrage it would have caused. "What an astounding pair of days."

Her smile ignited something in his chest. "So you've heard about our little wonder? The reverend said that you had seen the worst of our community, and now he was pleased that you were able to see us at our best."

"It is a fine thing."

"I'm so delighted for Grace House," she said.

Matthew let caution slip through his fingers. "I have a certain now-famous volume with me." He spoke the words quietly, his hand casually resting on his coat breast pocket. He knew exactly what he was doing, and it had the intended effect.

For a moment she seemed to hold her breath, and he

felt it in the skip of his heartbeat. "Is that wise?" she nearly whispered.

"I have the feeling it's best kept on my person for the time being. Imagine the spectacle should someone discover it."

Her eyes asked the question: *Will you reveal it?* What a strange thing it was to find himself in one of San Francisco's most enviable positions: knowing one of Stuart Waterhouse's secrets.

Chapter Fifteen

Surely, the Bible all but proved Stuart Waterhouse wrote the Bandit.

Ah, but Stuart still didn't know that Matthew was the one to bring the Bandit to life. Even if he never stooped to use them, holding such trump cards over Waterhouse was a rare moment indeed.

He'd rather have spent this moment in more private company with Georgia, but polite society had other plans. Instead, he found himself reduced to engaging Miss Waterhouse in a series of bland pleasantries as the other guests persisted in drifting in and out of their conversation. Stuart soared in for a moment, waving a white ribbon and pecking his sister on the cheek before a pair of his business associates whisked him away to meet someone "most important." After three more such distractions, Matthew finally secured a moment of privacy with her, and dived into the subjects he had wondered about for days.

"Why has Stuart never married?"

Miss Waterhouse put down the punch cup she was holding. "A bold question, Mr. Covington."

He tucked his hands in his pockets, rocking back on his heels. "Stuart is a bold man, Miss Waterhouse. And one of substantial wealth. Even with his...distinct character, he could have his choice of San Francisco's eligible young ladies."

Georgia turned her attention to an overlarge portrait of Stuart that hung beside the fireplace mantel. Posed in a thronelike chair beside a roaring fire, her brother looked so regal that the painting could have been hung on an ancient castle wall in Britain. The artist had also, however, captured the rebellious glint of Stuart's eyes. The sly turn of his mouth that let one know the man held a thousand secrets and wouldn't hesitate to use them.

"Stuart was almost married once," she said, her voice faraway as she touched the bottom corner of the frame. Matthew found the gesture surprisingly tender.

He liked that about her. Despite her brother's appetite for scandal, despite the fact that the floor beneath her feet and the clothes on her back and perhaps even the pearls at her neck had been very likely purchased with scandal, she wouldn't stoop to it.

Matthew held her eyes for a long moment, wanting to say so much more than was possible in the circumstances. "Still," he finally offered, "I believe marriage to be a fine and worthy institution."

"I agree." She gave a small smile and clasped her hands together. "I have seen the characters of many men highly improved by a fine marriage. I persist in my hope for Stuart."

He simply could not resist. Dropping his voice, he

inquired, "And of your own hope? If I were a less honorable man, I would not resist the temptation to ask you why it is that you haven't married."

Her smile became warm and broad. She laid her hands across her throat in a mock swoon. "Oh, then it is a good thing you are an honorable man, Mr. Covington. Your resistance is most appreciated."

It was the flash in her eyes that banished the last of his restraint. "Why is it you never married, Miss Covington?"

"What of your resistance?"

"It seems to have wandered off. I shall fetch it back…eventually."

"As well you should."

He waited for her to reply.

She didn't. She simply looked at him with a sly smile. Again he saw a hint of the very complex woman lurking under all that propriety. "Then I shall answer you…eventually," she murmured.

"But not now."

"No, Mr. Covington. Not now."

Somehow, her refusal to comply was even better than any answer she could have offered. Which was a daft thought. Georgia Waterhouse drove him to sheer lunacy. His previous night's work was proof of that.

Georgia fell back on her pillows, exhausted yet wide awake. *Such a day this has been, Lord.*

One of the two dogs that lived in the Waterhouse mansion home laid its head across the foot of the bed. More than a dozen years ago a San Francisco man had been crazed enough to declare himself emperor of the United States. He'd had two dogs, one named Lazarus, the other named Bummer. When the "Emperor" died in 1880, Stuart had gone out and purchased two dogs and given them the same names. Georgia pitied the beasts, which were caught up in her brother's endless plays for power, just as she was. "Lazarus, can you imagine such a thing? Money, nailed to trees with white ribbons? How do you suppose it was done?" She flipped herself around on the bed to face the dog, scratching the thin-faced hound between the ears. "How is it that no one saw it?"

Lazarus only moaned, then turned in circles to settle himself on the thick rug. Georgia flopped back, her arms spread across the plush covers. How had it been done? The scene unfolded in her imagination, materializing out of a gray fog in tiny details. He must be tall—of course he would be tall—and athletic. Nimble but very strong. He must have dressed in dark clothes to have moved about unnoticed, she imagined. Black? Brown? No, gray. A misty gray.

Where had the money come from? Locals always used gold coin—only Easterners had paper money. What did that mean? When had he decided to adopt Stuart's white strips?

She saw him in her mind's eye—a faceless, noble silhouette sliding in and out of the shadows. Broad-shouldered, dark-eyed. A brooding personality, perhaps. A man who had known some of life's pain, she decided, although she couldn't exactly say why. A man who knew the burden of command and the power of mercy.

A man too noble, too perfect to be real. Oh, what she would give to meet such a man. He must be out there, somewhere.

"Bless him, Father. Whoever he is, wherever he is, he is my hero. And, perhaps, Yours."

Hero. The Bandit lived. Georgia fell asleep imagining the mysterious details of the man who had stepped into the Bandit's boots and changed her world.

Chapter Sixteen

"Thank you. I should have been loath to miss this." Georgia smiled at Matthew Covington as they wandered about the art exhibit.

"You live too much at the mercy of Stuart's schedule," Mr. Covington offered. "Surely you could have your choice of escorts or husbands to free you from such a fate."

She wished he would move his focus from such a tender topic. "Mr. Covington," she replied, lightening her tone intentionally, "are you trying to tell me you've rediscovered your restraint? For I must confess, I see no evidence of it yet."

He grinned, caught in the act. He seemed to enjoy trying to get her to address the one question she had clearly told him she would not answer. Not anytime soon, at least. "I've seen no evidence of your response, either."

"And you shall not." She twirled the handle of her parasol. "As such, we are at an impasse. Shall we find a more pleasant topic?"

He paused, as if searching for one, but Georgia was quite

convinced he had a list of conversational gambits lined up in his head, each one designed to land up at the reason for her unmarried status.

He took a more direct tack than she would have expected. "Your brother seems quite intent on fostering our friendship." He chose his words carefully. They both knew it might have been more accurate to say, "Your brother throws us together at every opportunity, and I suspect invents his own."

Georgia opted for a sliver of truth. "Stuart believes you to be important."

"Stuart's fascination with the English is no secret. Perhaps all he admires is my pedigree."

She stared at him with narrowed eyes. "Would he be mistaken, Mr. Covington? Am I to discover that you are in fact a dishonorable Spanish spy? A notorious German, perhaps, gifted in deceptive accents?"

Matthew bowed. "A son of British soil, Miss Waterhouse, loyal to crown and country. Although I was thought to be good with voices as a child. Used to play endless tricks on the house staff and my brother." He tucked his hands in his pockets as they turned the corner. "But I'm afraid there's not much use for such antics in the running of a proper British enterprise. Stuart is right in one respect, I suppose—I am important." He did not say the word as if it were a compliment. Quite the opposite. "I've responsibilities bearing down upon me at every turn. Reputations to maintain. Honor to uphold. Profits to tend." He gave a small sigh. "I am continually aware that should Covington Enterprises pull up stakes, many would lose their livelihood." He stopped and gazed at her, as if it was something he hadn't intended to reveal. "I believe we were in search of a pleasant subject. This hardly qualifies."

"You feel your obligations keenly, don't you, Mr. Covington?"

"Yes, Miss Waterhouse, I suppose I do."

"A very good thing. I believe God wisely places men of high conscience in charge of such sizable burdens."

They stepped out onto a small terrace warmed by the sun. "You still think God wise, Miss Waterhouse? With all that you see of man's evil toward his fellow man?"

"Of course I think God wise," Georgia said, turning to gaze at a tall row of trees. The aging newspaper minion Stuart had sent along as a chaperone had disappeared into another exhibit hallway nearly a quarter of an hour before. "Man's evils are not God's doing, but only born of the wisdom of His gift of free will." She allowed herself to turn and look at Matthew, straight into his eyes. "No, Mr. Covington, I do not think God is at all pleased with San Francisco these days."

"You hold the scriptures in high regard, don't you?" He motioned for her to sit on a bench off to one side of the terrace.

"Indeed I do." She settled onto it, taking care to ensure space between them.

Mr. Covington glanced back at the terrace gate, as if confirming the predictable absence of their "guardian." "Very well, then. Last time, you asked me to read to you. I should like you to return the favor." He removed the tattered volume from his coat pocket and handed it to her. "Surely you have favorite passages."

* * *

"I know you must have one, if not several," Matthew continued when she hesitated.

Her eyes darted back and forth, as if this was something too private to do on a terrace bench. Did the words in that book really mean that much to her?

"I'm afraid it is on a subject most men find dull," she stated, sounding as if she knew it was a useless defense.

"I care not," he said quietly, refusing to let his gaze drop from the inviting puzzle of hers.

Finally, she let her eyes fall as she feathered through the pages. She cleared her throat and adjusted herself on the bench. "'If I speak with the tongues of men and of angels, but have not love,'" she began, and then read through a poetic passage about what real love was and why it mattered above all else.

He watched how her fingers held the page with affection. She did love these words.

"'Believeth all things, hopeth all things, endureth all things…'" She paused just a moment before she finished, "'Love never faileth.'" She shut the book with a tender gesture, running her finger along the slice as if to soothe it.

Georgia Waterhouse was an extraordinary woman. She was beautiful, but it was her inner strength, her fierce devotion and hope, that pulled at him. *Can I tell you how I admire you, or would it frighten you away?*

She held the book out to him and he took it, clasping her hands in his and holding them as long as he dared. She seemed small and fragile in that moment, and he wanted to draw a long silver sword and demand the world pay attention to her, to honor her for the wonder she was. "Thank you," he said, meaning so much more.

Late that night—so late, in fact, that it was actually the next morning—Matthew sat at his hotel bay window. Sleepless, he stared at the full, creamy moon and the shadows it cast over the city. He thought of her. He fingered the jagged hole in the Bible just as she had done, feeling for evidence of her touch. Her hands had felt so small in his.

He was taken with her.

He'd been taken with women before. Struck by some stunning beauty or a clever wit. But those were quick flashes of fireworks compared to the slow burn he now felt in his chest.

"Oh, you fancy her," his brother would often say of the latest object of Matthew's affections. He would not use that word now—*fancy* seemed nowhere near what he was feeling.

Of course, nothing could be less sensible. Even if Georgia—and he enjoyed thinking of her as "Georgia," not "Miss Waterhouse," even though he'd never take such liberties out loud—was the perfect woman for him, it could never be. He was an Englishman who must someday, sooner or later, return home. And even if Stuart Waterhouse might view it as the coup of the century, Matthew couldn't see himself taking Georgia away from either her brother or her beloved San Francisco. He wouldn't uproot her like that. Even if he managed to persuade her to move with him to England—which he suspected he could—eventually she would feel uprooted and displaced.

But he *was* taken with her. So much that he could scarcely picture himself leaving California under his own free will.

And that's what duty was about, wasn't it? Handling responsibilities even when doing so clashed with one's own free will.

Matthew stared about the room, looking at the trappings of his lifetime of obligation. Files upon files. Dignified coats and hats, letters of introduction, documents piling up beside books and ledgers. Only the whip and sword felt like his own possessions.

The whip and the sword.

Put that thought away right this moment, Matthew scolded himself. *You've no right to deceive her like that.* Still, he had already done so, hadn't he? He'd made the Bandit step into the real world. And it had nearly made her glow when she talked about it.

He bolted upright, the truth of it shocking him. Matthew Covington could never woo Georgia Waterhouse.

But he knew someone who could.

Chapter Seventeen

Dexter Oakman tucked his fingers in his vest pockets and smirked. "Genius."

"The last three issues alone have sent our second-quarter figures well above projections." Stuart laced his own fingers behind his head and leaned back in his chair. "A profit is a thing of beauty, Dex."

"You'll have more profits than you know what to do with after this new venture takes off, Mr. Waterhouse."

Stuart narrowed his eyes at Oakman. "Are we on track?"

"A few snags, but you'll have the cooperation you need by the end of the year."

That was good. Stuart needed the cooperation of certain well-placed individuals. Lots of well-placed individuals, if his final plan was to be realized. Labor and commerce were simply a means to an end, tools to exert or release pressure. A port's true value was in how it could be manipulated. And if Oakman could be believed, Stuart would be able to manipulate certain valuable markets to his whim by the year's end.

Oakman picked up a copy of the *Herald.* "So what of your real-life Bandit? Tossing money to the poor and making you look as if you called it down on the city's behalf. You want him to show up again?" Oakman turned and glanced at Stuart. "Or was it you who made him appear in the first place?"

It was, of course, the question everyone was asking. Had the *Herald* awakened a new hero, or simply installed one? Half the city—the optimists—believed the episodes had either driven a virtuous man to impersonate the Bandit, or had reported the Bandit's noble adventures under the guise of fiction to protect his secret identity. The other half of the city—the skeptics and cynics—believed the whole thing to be a clever stunt designed to sell papers.

Everyone had an opinion. It was the topic of endless discussions. Stuart, for the first time in a long time, waffled on which theory to encourage. Should he take credit for this new sensation, bolstering his reputation for sales genius? Or was the wiser move to play the noble card, humbly accepting his role in bringing out the city's inherent goodness?

It mattered not that he was, in truth, neither. Stuart had long discarded truth whenever there was profit to be made. And if profit came in the guise of a dashing swordsman invented by his sister, then who was he to turn it away?

Matthew heard the thick wooden doors shut behind him, blocking out the light as they closed. What sun still entered Grace House's tiny chapel was washed in a warm amber by the room's few small stained glass windows. The ornate churches in this city or in London never affected him. They were large and gracious and easy to dismiss as feats of architecture. This humble little chapel, however, seemed determined to seep into his bones. He'd walked through this chamber a dozen times during his visits to Grace House, but hadn't realized until this morning that he avoided lingering inside. It wasn't that he'd never had cause to be in here alone, but more that he unconsciously avoided it.

He had thought he was here to gain Reverend Bauers's partnership in a most unusual endeavor. That was why he'd come. But the sanctuary seemed to have an agenda all its own, as if it had been silently waiting for him to show up and walk into its grasp. Matthew felt ambushed by the extraordinary quiet. The room felt full and empty at the same time. He had the unsettling sensation of someone taking his insides and shaking them gently.

He breathed in the cool, distinct scent, a mix of candle wax, wood, and the smells of ritual he remembered from his infrequent visits to the cathedral in London. He'd shared his father's dislike of churches since he was young, being loath to suffer anything requiring quiet and stillness. Once, as a young lad, he'd slithered four pews away before his mother noticed his absence. Only Lady Hawthorne's shriek of surprise when young Master Covington's dusty, smiling face had peered up at her from below had given him away. His father had paddled him soundly—not for being disrespectful in church, but for sullying the family name.

Matthew figured out that day that the virtue extolled most in the Covington household was not piety, but propriety. In truth, his father cared little about the integrity of his conduct as long as its public appearance brought the family honor. If Matthew found a respectable way to enslave small children, he doubted his father would have raised an eyebrow. It all seemed so hollow.

Until Reverend Bauers and Georgia. Until here.

Matthew pulled the small Bible from his pocket. Such a tiny book with so much history and so much consequence. He'd grown uncomfortable with the thing. Like the chapel, it refused to remain a simple object. Instead, it seemed to become a force of nature. He found himself fingering the missing chunk, as Georgia had. He was constantly aware of the Bible's presence—the weight of it in his pocket, the texture of it in his hands, the space it occupied on his desk.

You're daft, Matthew told himself as he stared at the simple gold cross he had saved from theft. It disturbed him to have so personal a connection to so holy an object.

Something was here. Something he imagined others felt while gazing at the vaulted ceilings of cathedrals or the gilded intricacy of altars. It was something he heard in Georgia's voice. Something familiar, yet just beyond his recognition.

Something that was seeking him as fast as he was running from it.

He took another deep breath and closed his eyes, then found himself wishing Reverend Bauers had given him something else—*anything* else. Something that would remain a simple token. Which made no sense, for it was a tiny old book and he was a powerful British businessman.

Matthew groaned and leaned his forearms on the pew in front of him.

"So you *do* feel it," said a warm voice over his right shoulder. Matthew nearly leaped off the pew. Clergymen should not be able to sneak up on a man like that.

"I thought so," Reverend Bauers continued. He must have seen the alarm in Matthew's eyes, for he placed a hand on his shoulder and said, "Don't be alarmed. God's pursuit is nothing to be afraid of. Startling, perhaps, but not frightening."

Matthew didn't know what to say. He found he couldn't even be sure what Reverend Bauers was talking about. At least, that's what he told himself.

"Have you opened it, or have you just stared at it?"

"At what?" Matthew retorted, almost defensively.

Bauers smiled. "Come now, my son, what kind of man do you take me for? Do you think I give such gifts lightly?"

He knew. Somehow that made it far worse. Matthew made no reply.

Bauers sat down next to him and stared up at the cross. "What do you see up there?"

"I know what that is, but I tell you, Bauers, I'm no man of God."

The reverend laughed softly. "All men are of God, Covington. Some just refuse to recognize it. Some are born knowing it, others come to see it slowly and late in life. And then," he said, turning to look straight at him in a way that made Matthew's chest constrict, "there are the few whom God goes after with both barrels blazing."

He was certain there was no safe response to that.

"If you came to return the Bible because it disturbs you, I'll not take it back. Have you opened it at all?"

He could say yes. But truly, only Georgia had opened it. He'd held it, touched it, kept it near, but somehow had no desire to open it again, even to find the passage she had read. He felt as if he didn't know what would happen if he did.

"It won't bite you. Not, at least, in the way you think. I'd begin with Exodus, if I were you. I think you'll find Moses a man to your liking in many ways. And"—Bauers pointed to the missing chunk—"I think most of it's still there." The reverend's thick hand clasped Matthew's shoulder again and squeezed. "If you still find the need to rid yourself of it after that, we'll talk. But not a moment before. You're welcome at Grace House any day, at any time. Remember that."

He started to leave, but Matthew put a hand on his arm, stopping him. "Actually, I came for another reason. One you might scarcely believe."

Bauers raised an inquisitive eyebrow. "Well then, come into my study and let's have a talk."

Chapter Eighteen

Stuart ate his dinner with an air of deliberate calculation. This, Georgia recognized, was a sure sign of impending doom. He normally either relished his food or ignored it. Food was something he enjoyed when he felt good, or simply another task to accomplish when he felt overworked. It had become one of the easiest ways for Georgia to gauge her brother's volatile disposition. On the days when he ate carefully, she knew it could only mean he was plotting.

"Peach," he began as he pushed back his chair after the main course, injecting what Georgia imagined he thought was a casual tone into his voice. Did he have any idea how transparent he was? He tinkered with the heavy silver napkin ring at his left. "Are you happy?"

The question surprised her. It was an unusual opening for one of Stuart's controlling conversations. She had best tread very carefully with her answer.

"I'm delighted you ponder the issue," she said, avoiding the question. Years of debate with this king of secrets had built her skills in that department.

One hand went to his heart. "Of course I care about your happiness. We're all we have in the world."

If there ever was a classic Stuartism, "we're all we have in the world" would be it. It was his favorite saying when he wanted something from Georgia. Usually something large and questionable. "You, me, enormous material resources, a few dozen servants, and a host of admirers?" she countered. "We're hardly in seclusion, my dear brother."

He waved his hand and took a large swig from a crystal goblet. "I don't mean that. All this—" he gestured around the dining room "—is lovely, and you keep yourself enormously busy, but are you *happy?*"

She considered several options before deciding on a straightforward answer. "Yes, Stuart, I am. My world is not ideal, I grant you, but all things considered, I am very fond of my life."

He put the goblet back down on the table and ran his fingers over its silver trim. "You don't wish for more?" Stuart did have a gift for loaded questions.

Georgia thought about the humble mission, the families like Quinn's, and the abundance surrounding her here at the estate. More? She didn't need half of what she had. But that was Stuart at his core: always trying for more. More power, more influence, more money, more satisfaction, more *more.* She mused that if the Waterhouses ever commissioned a family crest, the motto need only be *More.*

"I should like to see more of my brother, but I fear I will have to wait in line behind his many minions." She hadn't entirely objected when he'd sent word about missing the exhibit at the conservatory. It had been a most extraordinary afternoon with Matthew Covington. Still, enough of those "coincidences" and there'd be talk. Stuart craved talk, but she did not.

He caught the hidden meaning in her reply. She was forcing him to be direct, and he knew it. He folded his napkin and laid it on the table. *Ah,* thought Georgia as she leaned her elbow on the arm of her chair, *now we get to the heart of the matter.*

"What do you think of our Mr. Covington?"

Georgia smiled.

"So you *do* like him!" Stuart pounced.

She held up her hand. "My smile, brother, comes from my amusement at having guessed your real question ten minutes ago. Honestly, do you find directness so appalling that you cannot even manage to be forthright with your own sister?"

Stuart planted his elbows on the table. "Where'd be the fun in that?"

"We'll never know until you try."

"We'll never know what you think of Covington until you answer my question," he insisted.

"He seems a good and decent man. And so very important. Not to mention so very British." Georgia gave him his answer, but threw Stuart's own agenda back at him in doing so.

"I could pursue Covington on your behalf, you know. I want you to be happy."

There it was. The tender, brotherly side the rest of the world never saw. People always asked her what it was that enabled her to endure all of Stuart's larger-than-life tendencies. That quiet tone of his voice let her know that despite his questionable methods, he often had shreds of good intentions. She believed he truly did want to see her happy, though his vision of what it took to achieve that was sadly distorted. After all, despite several past chances to wed her off to someone highly advantageous, he'd never done so against her wishes. Nor would he. He might try mightily to persuade her, but would never override her decision.

"I've no wish to haul off to England and play lady of the castle, Stuart. My home is here. Should I be swept off my feet anytime in the near future, however, I'll be sure you are among the first to know."

"Among?" he cried in mock alarm. "*Among* the first?"

"A lady does need a few secrets in this world," she teased, glad to have that rough patch over with. "Especially a Waterhouse."

He rose from his chair and went to pull out hers. As he did, he leaned over and pecked her on the cheek. "Speaking of secrets," he said into her ear, "I've a request to make of George."

Stuart shut the library doors a moment later. "We're getting near the end of the quarter and I need a firecracker of a Bandit episode."

Georgia gazed up at him. He looked so much older when he slicked his hair back, close to his head like that. It made him look sleek and severe. Stuart's personality almost demanded a headful of unruly curls, not the razor-straight white-blond hair they'd both received from their mother. Their father had had dark, wavy hair. Stuart had his eyes, but mostly her efforts to see her father reflected in Stuart went unrewarded. He neither looked like him nor acted like him. Still, Stuart was her brother, and no matter how much he liked to exploit the phrase, he was indeed "all she had in the world."

"I think you overstate my...*George's* influence," she

replied. "It wasn't the words that created the sensation. It was whoever duplicated them in real life."

"Never underestimate the power of the word, Peach. It's all in the words." He tapped a succession of books on the shelf behind him.

"Meaning?"

"Meaning give our mysterious imitator something to work with," Stuart replied. "Write an episode that just begs to be imitated."

Georgia sat down. Write an episode designed to be acted out? The idea felt absurd. Why not simply hand out white ribbons with each issue of the *Herald* tomorrow? Goodness, she'd best not suggest that—Stuart might actually seize the idea. She stopped and stared at him. "You're serious. You actually want to encourage such a thing?"

"You've been encouraging people to do noble deeds your entire life. Why stop now?"

There was some odd logic to his notion, but it still felt horribly wrong. Unscrupulous and manipulative. "Stuart, I couldn't."

He pointed at her. "You could. And that's what scares you. You've hidden behind your lack of influence for too long, Peach. Now you've got it. Use it."

She didn't know how to respond. "*George* has it," she replied, mostly because she couldn't craft another answer.

"What's in a name? 'That which we call a rose by any other name would smell as sweet.' Shakespeare said that. And that man knew the power of words. Come on, Peach. Stir up a crop of heroes. Who knows what will happen if you do?"

Who knows indeed, Georgia thought.

Chapter Nineteen

Sitting at her bedroom desk, Georgia stared at her pen. Could she stir up a crop of heroes? It didn't even need to be a crop, did it? Look at what just one man did at Grace House. Then again, did she know it was one man? Who knew anything about how the white ribbons and money had appeared? She thought about Reverend Bauers's glowing face as he'd tucked the money into the mission safe. About the children playing with the white ribbons. She hadn't done any of it, but she'd inspired it. Could she inspire more?

Lord, Georgia prayed, clutching her pen inside her folded hands, *I'm toying with fire. Guide my words. I know You have the power to transform men and to work wonders, but I've no wish to play God. Shut this door if this is not Your will, and end this charade before anyone is hurt.* She waited for a sense of danger, an urge to halt, to overtake her. Instead, stories began to weave themselves together in her head. *If You have something astounding in mind, Lord, then grant me courage. I'll go where You want, but stay beside me.*

She stared at the blank sheet of paper. What would be easy to bring to life? Something common. Something everyday that could be swiftly transformed into something wondrous. What was commonplace to people in need? An image began to form in her mind's eye. Georgia took a deep breath and wrote.

> "The fog swirled thick and gray around him. The Bandit shrugged off the evening's chill as he watched the men unload the ship. They chatted casually, unaware of the priceless nature of the boxes they hauled."

Matthew woke from a delightfully sound sleep. He dressed quickly in an unassuming coat and trousers—a step or two down from his usual impressive attire—and snatched a trio of apples from the bowl on the sitting room table.

Thompson looked up from polishing Matthew's boots. He raised a salt-and-pepper eyebrow at the plain dress of his master. Matthew raised an eyebrow back, then juggled the three apples for a moment before sending one sailing in Thompson's direction.

The old man calmly caught the fruit, as if he'd been expecting it for hours. "Feeling fit this morning, sir?"

Matthew bit into the one of the remaining apples in his hands. "Indeed I am."

"May I ask why so casual?"

"No," said Matthew simply, suddenly wondering why in his seven-and-twenty years it hadn't occurred to him to say such a thing before. "You may not." It sounded rather petulant, but directness was surprisingly effective against an adversary as wily as Thompson.

Matthew started to say something such as, "I'll be inspecting some holdings until well into the afternoon," but stopped himself. He wasn't required to explain himself at all, was he? Surely civility and decorum required such a thing, but under the circumstances…

"I'm off," he said, taking another bite, as if the two words were all the explanation required.

He strode down the hallway, imagining Thompson's jaw hanging slack behind him. It probably wasn't—there was a good chance Thompson wasn't even surprised by Matthew's unusual behavior—but it was much more amusing to think otherwise.

It had been so easy to arrange. Reverend Bauers had proved an adept accomplice, with a dozen ideas on how to give the Bandit a life of his own South of the Slot. Anonymity and money rendered such things highly doable. Matthew had the easier role: secure the needed funds without attention—which generally meant putting a sizable dent in his own personal travel allowance—and then pass them on to the reverend. The funds changed hands two or three times—each with a small cost for the transaction, unsurprisingly—in order to ensure the proper amount of confusion, and the intended target received money from a variety of untraceable sources.

Fortunately, Matthew thought with a smile as he stood several blocks away from the mercantile that was their first target, *the reverend seems as skilled a prankster as I.* For a man of the cloth, he got a very pirate-worthy gleam in his eye when he smiled.

The neighborhood grocery market inhabited a wide, solid building whose front opened out onto an enormous porch-like space. Its owner was a stoic Italian named Vincenzo Trivolatti, who had come to San Francisco to seek his fortune, and found love in the process, marrying a local Irish girl. Where Vincenzo was all business, his wife, Irene, was all heart, or so Reverend Bauers said. Aiding the cause of the Bandit, provided it proved sufficiently profitable, would appeal to both their sensibilities. It seemed an ideal match.

Despite the earliness of the hour, a crowd had already begun to form amid the neat stacks of produce and goods under the market's front awning. It was Friday, market day, and the neighborhood grocery would be bustling even under normal circumstances. Matthew doubted Trivolatti would ever know the likes of this day again. He'd seen to that.

It had taken only three hours to arrange the details. One hour before opening, a young boy was sent with a letter to the Trivolatti home, disclosing two impending arrivals at the market. The first would be a supply of white cloth strips. Reverend Bauers had prayed that God would prevent all medical emergencies as he and Matthew shredded Grace House's existing bandage supply to produce the needed tokens. Matthew had thought to himself amusingly that at the rate he was going, several of the hotel bedsheets might have to go missing in order for him to restock Grace House's medical stores. Bauers predicted that the ribbon delivery alone should catch Irene's undivided attention. No one South of the Slot had escaped hearing about the Bandit's first adventure.

The second delivery, intended to secure Mr. Trivolatti's cooperation, was a supply of funds delivered by secured guard as a deposit for the day's tally. Matthew's inspection of the Covington Enterprises shipping logs had given him enough of a working knowledge of the cost of daily goods in San Francisco. With a few simple calculations, he could guarantee that the amount delivered would be more than enough to ensure Trivolatti a healthy day's profit. The letter instructed the grocer to take no payment for any order placed today, and that if the funds provided did not cover the orders placed—which Matthew predicted would be highly unlikely, but given the speed of dock gossip, not impossible—to write down the remaining balance and it would be paid the following morning by similar messenger. Instead of demanding payment, Vincenzo was to simply hand a white ribbon to his customers and inform them that the Bandit had bought their groceries.

Irene, a generous and highly religious woman, would no doubt keep her eye on the entire proceedings. She was just the sort of principled individual who would rather die than see such a noble act abused. Times, however, were tough, and she was only one woman, so just in case greed should rear its ugly head, a banking clerk had been anonymously hired to keep tabs on the day's event. Matthew didn't much care for the idea of Irene having to single-handedly ward off a mob of opportunists. Matthew would have loved to have had the Bandit standing guard, sword gleaming in the sunshine from atop a nearby building, but such a thing was neither practical nor advisable. It was not only beyond outlandish, but Matthew's arm had not yet gained back its full strength, and should the Bandit need to swoop down and defend the poor Trivolattis, Matthew—

or any mere mortal, for that matter—would hardly be up to the task.

Matthew and Reverend Bauers had opted for the power of words instead. “You will be watched,” the note had concluded, “for the Bandit rewards his partners, but hunts his adversaries without mercy.” True, it had been rather dramatic, but wasn’t drama the point of it all?

Legends could hardly afford to be subtle. Stuart Waterhouse had taught him that.

Chapter Twenty

Matthew leaned against a building a block away, nondescript in his workman's clothes, and observed. An old woman called out grateful exclamations as she left the mercantile, clutching the white ribbon to her breast. She spoke in Italian, but no translation was needed. Waving to a small boy across the street, she told him something in rushed words and shooed him away, presumably to spread the news. Other families came trotting up the street, nearly running in their hurry to take advantage of the windfall. Another woman took Mr. Trivolatti's face in her hands and kissed him on both cheeks when he handed her the ribbon. Mrs. Trivolatti protested at great length, only to laugh, hug her husband and enjoy their role in the spectacle.

This went on for over an hour as Matthew watched, the reactions of surprised and grateful families making him feel like a king. He had done it for Georgia, but felt such a deep personal satisfaction that he wondered which of them would enjoy it more.

When Reverend Bauers came walking down the street

midmorning, exactly as planned, the ruckus erupted all over again. Men and women huddled around him to tell him the news, and he feigned surprise comparable to the best London actors. Matthew laughed to himself, thinking he had chosen a highly capable coconspirator in the lively round man.

The hush that suddenly fell over the crowd caught Matthew by surprise. It was a few seconds before he realized the market had fallen into prayer. In the quiet, he found he could hear the reverend's words clearly.

"Most Holy Father, we are overwhelmed in thanks to You this day. We bless You for how You have provided for Your faithful. In Your wisdom and mercy, You have sent us a champion. A soldier of justice we have not seen. Bless Your servant, this Bandit, and strengthen him with the thanksgiving of those he has helped. Reward him for honoring Your calling. Protect him for future deeds of justice and mercy. May we remain grateful and hopeful, and may we continue to trust in You, because of the things You have done today." As the reverend raised his hand to pronounce "Amen," a cheer went up through the small crowd.

Matthew stood there, locked in place by the words. Bauers knew he would be within earshot. The reverend must have chosen his prayer as much for Matthew's sake as for the crowd's.

He'd called him a servant. As though what he was doing was some sort of holy mission, not just one man's ill-advised attempts at heroism.

As though it hadn't been Matthew's idea.

The concept shook him to the core. This was little more than a prank, not some crusade. He wasn't even sure it fell under the category of "good deeds." He was, when one got right down to it, showing off for a girl. One could hardly call that divine intervention. More to the point, one could hardly take marching orders from a God one wasn't even certain existed in the first place.

Matthew shook his head, checked his watch and headed back to the hotel by a side street. California was proving to be a most unsettling place. The sooner he got back to precise, well-behaved ledgers and numbers, the better.

"Are your inspections proving satisfactory?" Thompson droned as he brushed off Matthew's coat and adjusted the lapel later that week.

"Yes, quite."

"And you've fully recovered from your injuries?" Again, the dry tone of a man compiling facts. Which was always reason to suspect Thompson. He collected facts the way a boy with a slingshot collected small stones—as tiny weapons capable of great impact.

"Nearly," Matthew said carefully, flexing his arm and twisting his wrist this way and that. He suffered an occasional sting if he hit the wrong angle, but within the week he should be up to speed. The scar was quite evident. He was grateful life rarely afforded him a reason to roll up his sleeves. The thing looked like it belonged on a war hero, not a well-bred gentleman.

Thompson had tried valiantly to repair the slashed coat, but it had been beyond helping. No matter, the finding, measuring and ordering of a new jacket had given Thompson something to do other than gather facts on Matthew.

"Your father will be expecting a report next week," Thompson said, as dryly as ever. He was a master at dropping verbal bombs without flinching.

A report. There was much to report, but not much that Matthew could be certain about yet. His review of the books had proved them clean. Exceedingly clean. Unnaturally clean, which had given rise to Matthew's suspicion that things were not what they seemed. In a town where corruption was the local currency, Covington Enterprises should not have such pristine books. A certain amount of "greasing the wheel"—he'd heard the term recently—would have to go on in any commercial enterprise as large as Covington. Yet everything lined up in the records. There was not even a simple addition error in sight.

It was, in Matthew's opinion, too perfect to be believed. He could not shake the nagging suspicion that things had been cleaned up for his viewing. Some of that was to be expected, of course, for no one hauled himself across the Atlantic by surprise. The staff had had several months' notice of Matthew's arrival. Surely they'd tidied up a bit. But this was altogether something else. Something he couldn't quite yet name.

How to report as much to his father? Should he communicate his hunch? No, Matthew preferred to delay his report until he had a better sense of Covington Enterprises' true workings. And that would take time. It would take making friends, asking around and observing carefully. One could hide shady dealings for a handful of weeks, while the master was in town, but sooner or later "business as usual" would emerge. Not that Matthew minded extending his visit. The brisk air of San Francisco suited him far better than

London's cold, damp atmosphere. As did lots of other city amenities. And citizens.

As if to underscore the city's attractions, Thompson held out a sheet of paper Matthew recognized to be Stuart's personal stationery. "You've received an invitation to dine at the Waterhouse estate tomorrow evening. Shall I send your acceptance?" A wry taunt underlay Thompson's words.

Matthew had thought through his response earlier, for he was sure he'd receive another invitation from the Waterhouses. Stuart was doing a masterful job of controlling their social interaction, but it was time Matthew took the upper hand.

"No, Thompson, I'm afraid I'll need to decline. I've a business engagement to attend to that evening." He didn't, but one could be easily arranged. "Would you send an invitation for both Mr. and Miss Waterhouse to join me at the hotel for tea on Monday afternoon? It's high time I return their gracious hospitality, and I've found the Palace's tea service quite up to snuff."

Thompson raised an eyebrow. *Ha!* thought Matthew to himself, *surprised you, didn't I?* It gave him no small pleasure to foil Thompson's assumptions every once in a while. The man was simply incorrigible when he was right all the time. And he was, most of the time.

But the invitation had other advantages as well. Matthew had just read today's newspaper. The *Herald* had reported the incident at Trivolatti's grocery in glowing terms. And this week's Bandit episode continued in the same vein—as a matter of fact, it simply *begged* to be brought to life. It would be so easy to arrange, it was nearly an invitation to do so. A dare, even. As such, Matthew and the reverend had a little work to do, and Sunday night was going to be a busy one. What better way to reward a hard night's heroism than to discuss it with Stuart and Georgia the next day? To ensure a view to her reaction since he'd not seen her after the grocer's event? It was too enticing to resist.

Chapter Twenty-One

Sister Charlotte was exactly the kind of person Georgia wished to seek out for her odd confidence. The tall, energetic nun had a personality—and a past—worthy of newspaper headlines. She'd enjoyed a very successful career on the stage until she had captured the heart of a theater patron, who'd married her and given her a social life nearly as grand and public as her stage career. For a few years, Charlotte had been the darling—and perhaps the target—of San Francisco society. Then her husband had taken ill suddenly and died, ending yet another distinctive chapter of her life. Jaws of people all across the city had dropped when she joined the Sisters of Notre Dame and became a nun.

Her dramatic life made Sister Charlotte a unique woman. Highly independent for one having taken the vows. A sort of morally upright Stuart, Georgia thought, in that she had little concern for what others thought of her. She took care of people others would overlook or shun. Even before she'd joined the order, she'd engaged in what Stuart had called "taking in strays," for Charlotte often had a surprising spectrum of characters come to live on her palatial estate. The list of entertainers, scoundrels, hard cases and celebrities who'd enjoyed her hospitality would fill a year's worth of Stuart's gossip columns.

Charlotte cared about people, period. She had always been quite vocal about caring for God, too, which was why Georgia found it odd that people were suspicious of her "conversion." Sister Charlotte hadn't converted at all, merely formalized a strong faith into a holy office. Even in a stark black habit, she simply was what she was—a big-hearted woman who felt God gave her lots of things so she could share them with the world.

As she walked down the street from Grace House toward the convent a few blocks away, Georgia decided some of the Bandit's outlandish drama must have come from her image of Sister Charlotte. Were she male, Charlotte would have been a logical candidate for the Bandit, Georgia was certain. She wasn't sure some of San Francisco society didn't suspect Charlotte, anyway—she was just the kind of woman to dress as a man and run around saving the world.

Hardly the kind of wise old sage one turned to for advice.

Then again, it was hardly the normal kind of advice Georgia was seeking. To be truthful, she wasn't at all sure of what she was doing, or why she was doing it. She only knew she had to talk to someone, and this was not a subject for Reverend Bauers's ears. Or any other pastor's, even though several churches supported Grace House, and she was a member of one of them. This was a female matter. Or more precisely, a matter of female faith, which, as Georgia saw it, made it suited to Sister Charlotte's "unique" perspective.

The nun offered Georgia tea in a corner of the convent gardens. Even now, without her legendary luxury, she was a delightful hostess. Despite a habit of repeating herself, she tended brilliantly to all the little details of a warm welcome.

The tea was lovely, the setting peaceful, but never bringing up Stuart Waterhouse's name was the most refreshing thing, as far as Georgia was concerned. Charlotte seemed to see her for the woman she was, not just as the sister of the city's most prominent publisher. Charlotte was one of only a handful of people who did so, which made it a wonderful thing indeed.

"It seems to me," she said, leaning conspiratorially toward Georgia as she poured more tea, "that you're not here to discuss the bandage supply or parish funding for Grace House. Oh, no. You've got more on your mind, if I daresay so, and I do always dare to say what I think, all the time." She laid her hand gracefully on Georgia's arm. "What can I do for you, Georgia?"

"I...I have a problem of a most delicate nature."

Charlotte's smile was as quick as it was warm. "I thought so. Tell me, is it a matter of the heart, or a matter of the soul? Those are the only things that really count, you know."

"I believe it to be a matter of the heart, Sister, but I must confess that I am not at all sure."

"Sure?" she said, picking up a small biscuit. "Who is certain about any such thing?" She took a bit of the biscuit, then folded her long slim fingers together across her lap. "So now, what is this matter which you suspect to be of the heart?"

"I find myself enormously taken with a particular man." She said it quietly, as if the trees might repeat the news if she spoke too loudly.

"Goodness, that is a matter indeed." The nun looked at her with serious eyes. "Are you in love?"

"I don't believe I can be," Georgia said.

"Nonsense," countered Charlotte, sitting back in the bent-willow garden chair. "All of God's creatures are capable of love."

"I cannot love this man," Georgia explained, feeling her cheeks grow hot with embarrassment, "because he does not exist."

That stopped Sister Charlotte dead in her tracks. "Not exist? Is this like something from one of those novels—all swashbuckling romance without a hint of how to get along in the real world?"

Georgia gulped. The Bandit was a swashbuckling novel in Stuart's eyes. She hadn't counted on such an attitude from a veteran of the theater. She'd expected Sister Charlotte, despite her current austerity, to understand the power of imagination. "It is a fascination of a…literary sort…I suppose."

Sister Charlotte took a drink of tea. "Robin Hood!" she declared, as if it solved everything.

"Robin Hood?"

"I was smitten with him when I was younger. Read everything I could get my hands on about him. Dreamed up a picture in my head, his voice, the way he walked. Suddenly, no man on earth could compare. There were men who looked like my Robin Hood. Men who walked like him, but no one who came close to being who I'd created in my mind." She tapped the crisp white rim of her veil. "You've got a Robin Hood in your head, don't you?"

Georgia was quite sure her mouth was open. "In a manner of speaking, I suppose you are right."

"Of course I'm right. I could see it in your eyes the moment I said it. And you think you're the only woman to do something so outlandish? Women with fine imaginations have found themselves in your slippers more times than I can count. And we all think we're insane for doing it. You were smart to come to me, you know." She leaned in closer and lowered her voice. "Not everyone understands these things. Especially here."

Now there was an understatement. Georgia was quite sure she didn't understand a shred of her current emotional predicament. "But you understand?" she said, not caring how relieved she must sound.

"Completely. But I doubt it's Robin Hood who has your attention, my dear. I suspect he's a little antiquated for your taste. What tale has captured you?"

"Well..."

Charlotte's eyes widened. "Wait! Say not another word! How could I not see it? How could I not have guessed? The Bandit. It's the Bandit, isn't it?"

Georgia could only nod.

"Yes," the nun said, a knowing smile creeping into her violet eyes, "I read it. We are allowed newspapers, you know. And I might have smuggled it in if we didn't." She chuckled. "All the world wants to know where your brother got him, but I suspect even you wouldn't divulge that now, even to me?"

"No." Georgia found it hard to choke out the single syllable. Charlotte seemed to find her strange delusion so ordinary, so completely understandable, that Georgia felt as if her ability to breathe had just this moment returned.

"You have taste, I'll grant you that much." Charlotte sighed. "He'd be a rare find, our Bandit, if he walked into the real world."

"Yes…" Georgia kept waiting for more words to form, but she was stuck with single syllables for the moment.

"Of course, he *has* now, hasn't he? Shown up in a few dramatic encounters of late. That does complicate things. I can see where you'd be in a bit of a state. It's not every day that the man of your daydreams appears in reality." She tsked, pouring more tea. "Presents quite a challenge." She stopped, as if a thought had suddenly occurred to her. "Have you *seen* him? Our Bandit? Has he come to you? I couldn't think of anything more romantic, really."

"No. He hasn't."

The sister draped herself across the table, leaning on one elbow. She assessed Georgia with narrowed eyes—dramatic, violet eyes that Georgia imagined had sent more than one man's heart into spasms. "That's not the issue, really, is it? There's more to this than our mysterious hero."

Again, Georgia felt herself blush. "An ordinary man," she began, but then corrected herself. "Actually, he's far from ordinary, but he's not—"

"Say no more," interjected Charlotte, throwing her hands up in a melodramatic gesture. "Now I see your pickle. And why you came to me. How did I fall for Robert Brownstone when I had all of the stage's handsome heroes fawning at my feet? How does one make a life in the real world when the fantasy is so very enticing?" She pointed a finger at Georgia. "You're a sharp one, Miss Waterhouse. You know where to go for good advice, and that's half the battle, I always say. Our real-world hero—is he sensible? Does he suit you?"

"Not at all. In that I mean I see little hope for any future between us. I'm not even sure I want one." Suddenly, Georgia found her tongue. "He has many wonderful qualities, and I do believe he is fond of me, but there are so many obstacles."

"Ha!" Charlotte exclaimed. "What would love be without obstacles? No fun at all, to hear my dear late Robert tell it. God is at His best overcoming obstacles. We'd know nothing of our Lord without the teaching of our own mistakes." She settled herself in her chair. "Now let's be practical for a moment. Have you kissed him?"

Georgia nearly dropped her teaspoon.

"Well, it's a perfectly sensible question, given the circumstances. Have you?"

She shook her head.

"Good. Don't kiss him—or let him kiss you—unless you're absolutely sure. Take it from a woman of the stage, young lady, a man's kiss can be a distraction. It can hide far too much. You'll always know a true kiss when you feel it, but a proper young lady such as yourself doesn't always know a false kiss when it comes her way." The woman drew up her chin with an authoritative air. "Only the stage can teach you that."

Georgia came away from her meeting with the sure impression that she had made a good choice in confiding in Sister Charlotte. And that the Sisters of Notre Dame didn't know half of what they had in her. Odd as she was, Sister Charlotte was the perfect blessing. Perhaps the only sort of woman to understand the circumstance in which Georgia found herself.

She was also quite sure that whatever advice she'd received on the perils of insincere kisses, she was in no danger—immediate or otherwise—of having such a challenge thrust upon her. Tea at the Palace Hotel, even if Stuart should pull another of his disappearing acts, was hardly the place where men ravished women. True, the hotel had a reputation for hosting all sorts of characters, but the more unsavory of the lot rarely showed up for tea.

Chapter Twenty-Two

"Come now, you insufferable rascals, get on with it." Matthew could hardly believe his present circumstances. The Covington heir was, at the moment, dangling a jar of camphor through a hole he'd recently cut in the top of a chicken crate.

A crate of chickens. Does a proper English gentleman allow himself to be found standing among crates of chickens at two in the morning, engaged in the questionable act of drugging poultry?

Well, thought Matthew, *not if he can help it. I'd have a time explaining myself if I got caught, now wouldn't I?*

Of course, Reverend Bauers's pacing at the back of the stockyards wasn't helping to maintain calm. Even in the dim moonlight, Matthew could see the sweat beading on the clergyman's bald head. Not that he wasn't sweating himself. He swung the rope holding the jar again, splashing a little of the liquid on the crate floor. How had he made it this many years without realizing how dreadful chickens smelled? "You all smell so lovely when roasted," he crooned to the birds, "but I can't say the same for your present state. Breathe deeply, ladies, I can't stand here all night. Take lovely little deep chicken sighs, if you will. That's it…"

As one wobbly white hen sat down and settled her head, another brown-speckled hen followed suit. A third slumped in a corner. "There we go."

"You're sure this will work?" Reverend Bauers's agitated whisper came from somewhere behind him. "No one became suspicious when you bought so many chickens?"

Of course he wasn't sure it would work. Using the liquid on a handkerchief to drug the family cat so it could be locked in his father's armoire was one thing. Buying six different crates of chickens at three different places, and arranging for them all to be delivered to a fourth location, was one thing. Drugging said cratefuls of chickens to quiet them for a stealthy journey to the center of town was proving quite another.

He should have stuck with eggs.

The eggs were easy. Supplying a neighborhood with eggs for their Easter breakfast simply meant arranging for baskets of them to be tied with white ribbons and delivered before Easter. He could have recreated the Bandit's latest exploit without breaking a sweat—in fact, Matthew half worried someone else might try to play Bandit and beat him to it.

Chickens to go along with the eggs, now *that* presented a challenge.

More challenge than Matthew liked, to be honest. He'd thought the idea of drugging the chickens so that they could be quietly transported was brilliant. The chickens, however, weren't feeling that cooperative. It was taking twice the time he'd calculated for the feathered little beasts to fall asleep. If he used stronger solution, the Bandit's gift to the community might be crates of chicken carcasses. Which was why Matthew Covington found himself dashing among crates of chickens at two in the morning, waiting for them to fall asleep. His father would be in convulsions if he knew.

To think this was the easiest part of the plan.

Reverend Bauers was just beginning to beseech the Lord for sleeping chickens when the last of the plump little darlings slumped into a heap and Matthew reeled in the jar. "Got it!" For the next half hour, he and the reverend worked feverishly to tie white ribbons to one leg of each sleeping bird. It proved a ridiculously complicated task. Finally, they were ready. The Reverend then took off in the direction of a large cart happily lent by the Trivolatti store. They'd sent a note the night before, asking to have the cart waiting empty on a particular street corner. The Trivolattis had been told to leave the cart unmanned, but no one suspected that would be the case; a Bandit sighting presented far too great a temptation.

Which was why Matthew's new disguise proved such a blessing. As he leaped out of the shadows dressed in a gray shirt, dark trousers, black hat with a single white feather, and black mask—the Bandit's known costume—Matthew simply nodded at the awestruck young man who handed over the reins.

Yes, the Bandit wore his signature costume now. And no one could have predicted how that came to be.

Thompson, in an act that would shock Matthew until his dying day, had appeared with the garb two evenings before. How the valet had figured out his role, Matthew didn't know.

Nor would he ever, for when he found his tongue again and asked Thompson how he'd guessed, the man had only produced the widest smile Matthew had ever seen and said absolutely nothing.

Thompson—*Thompson,* of all people—knew.

Thompson approved.

Wilder still, he conspired! If Matthew was looking for signs that playing the Bandit was his destiny, then one could find no greater endorsement than Thompson's cooperation.

"It is my duty to see you properly dressed," his valet had said, after laying out the dark trousers, charcoal-gray shirt, wide-brimmed black hat and outlandish white feather—cleverly removable for discreet missions. The design of the Bandit's wardrobe had not been Thompson's; the outfit had been detailed in a recent episode in the *Herald.* Its execution, however, was extraordinary. Matthew could only imagine what it had taken for Thompson to see to its secret assembly.

True to the old man's impeccable sense of detail, Matthew noted a few smart embellishments. The pants had dozens of useful pockets and specially sewn loops to hold a unique belt. Rather like a holster, but much more elegant, the latter held both Matthew's sword and his whip. The mask, perhaps the most difficult thing of all, was outstanding. A thin leather caplike contraption, with a panel that folded down over the eyes, close to the head and neatly under the hat. The outfit was half pirate, half Musketeer and wholly perfect.

"I—I've no words," Matthew had stammered as he took the clothes from the grinning old man.

"Then none are needed," Thompson had said simply, as if the exchange were as common as a daily bath.

Something indescribable had stirred in Matthew when he put the clothing on. As if a new man—a bold, invincible spirit—had slid from the shell of the duty-bound accountant. It was as if, before, Matthew had been imitating the Bandit. But once wearing the disguise, he *became* him.

And the Bandit could do anything, including wrangle chickens.

One hoped.

By four-thirty in the morning, the crates of quieted chickens had been loaded onto the cart. Matthew sat in the driver's seat, convincing himself that the Bandit could drive a buckboard wagon at considerable speed just as easily as Matthew had raced his father's best carriage around the stable yards.

He edged the cart forward and heard a few clucks of protest from waking chickens. Now was the time.

He was just about to spur the team of horses forward when he felt Reverend Bauers's hand clasp his right foot. The clergyman bent his head and rested both hands on Matthew's shiny black boot.

"Bless this man and his bravery, Father. See that this food finds its way into homes to honor you, just as this man honors Your call to service. These creatures are given to those who dearly need food. And dearly need hope. Let us never forget Your hope and the sacrifice You paid for our sins. Protect this man with the might of Your hand as he serves Your people. Amen."

Matthew once again found his tongue tangled by the reverence this man seemed to place upon his ridiculous deeds.

He was play-acting for his own vaunted reasons, not "saving" anyone. Still, something tugged at him, that same sense of being caught up in something larger than himself or his faulty motives. Tonight, he felt as if he were a shred of the hero Reverend Bauers seemed to make him.

Was it selfish to hope that Georgia Waterhouse would hold the deed in the same regard? If he was truly going about God's business, then he had no right to twist such service to catch the eye of a woman. Still, if God was as all-seeing as Bauers claimed him to be, then surely He was already aware of Matthew's baser motive. *And is most likely angered by it,* he thought. *It's a wonder I'm not struck down by lightning this very second.*

Wouldn't that roast the chickens? He laughed, thinking how they might at least smell better. As Reverend Bauers called "Godspeed!" Matthew pulled the cart into the street and spurred the horses into a quick trot.

After so much planning, the execution seemed to fly by in a matter of heartbeats. Dressed as the Bandit, he drove squarely into the middle of a predetermined intersection. They'd chosen one in the center of the neighborhood, where it would soon be noticed. He suspected he'd already been, even at that hour.

He quickly leaped from the cart and sprinted to the back, where the crates of sleeping chickens stood beside several boxes of eggs.

Now for the finishing touch. The last dollop of drama to take this episode from anecdote to legend. And the first test of Matthew's healed arm. With a deep breath, he pulled his whip from the loop on his trousers and clasped the handle.

Shifting it back and forth a time or two, he let his arm recall its weight and rhythm. Then, with enormous satisfaction, he swung it back and cracked it several times just above the chicken crates, sending the sound ringing through the deserted intersection in a way that was sure to call attention.

Matthew waited only one second before dashing off into the darkness, where a hidden set of clothes waited to usher him back into obscurity.

Chapter Twenty-Three

"It sounds calamitous," Matthew said as he poured a second cup of tea. "I do wish I'd been around to see it. Chickens? Really?" It felt ridiculous to pretend ignorance.

"Hordes of them," Georgia said, a laugh stealing into her voice. Matthew could see the amusement in her face as she described the wild scene. "They were still running everywhere, even hours later, trailing white ribbons, feathers flying. I don't think I've ever seen anything like it."

"How on earth does one get that many chickens beribboned and into the center of town undetected?" he asked, doing his best to sound astonished. He forced himself, for discretion's sake, to interject a shred of disapproval into his voice. In truth, it was more than just an effort to maintain his disguise; some part of him wanted to see what Georgia would do if pressed to defend the Bandit.

"It seems to me," she replied, as she set down her teacup, "that we are dealing with a most extraordinary fellow. Quite resourceful. Very noble, but I suppose a bit reckless by some standards."

Very noble, resourceful and a bit reckless. It was funny to hear such words. If God himself had asked Matthew how he would like to be remembered, those were very nearly the attributes he would cite. And here Georgia was mentioning that about the Bandit—who was, and was not, Matthew Covington. It was an odd and yet powerful sensation.

Made more so by what Matthew could see lingering in Georgia's eyes—an admiration for the recklessness. An admiration that came close to affection for the dashing hero her brother had dreamed up. What a heady concept that was.

Which made Matthew wonder…had Stuart dreamed up the Bandit just for her? A prank to please his sister? Matthew scorned the idea of playing upon her sensibilities like that…until he realized that what he was doing was not much different.

It stung.

The Bandit was reckless. Matthew Covington could not be. Dashing midnight bravery was a luxury for imaginary men, not Covingtons.

Still, as he looked at her there, glowing in a butter-colored gown that set off her glistening gold hair, he knew he would do it again. To watch her talk of it with that look on her face, to know that she held a part of him—even an invented part—in such esteem, was enough.

It would have to be, wouldn't it? There could be no future between them. The cold gray halls of England would stifle her, and he was duty-bound to return home soon, no doubt to marry an appropriate woman of his mother's choosing.

"The eggs will help make a festive Easter for the children. I've always loved Easter eggs. I think childhood traditions are the ones we most remember," Georgia said, smiling as she evidently recalled another detail from the scene. "What are the Easter traditions at the Covington household? Do you remember any from your youth?"

Matthew toyed with his spoon. "There was always an enormous fair. There was an egg tradition there, too. Blindfolded men and women would dance across the street and try to avoid the eggs placed in their path. Many a good pair of shoes came to ruin on those days. My father took me to Spain several times to the bullfights that happen there at Easter. Ghastly business, really. I much preferred the fair at home. One could have far more fun with far less mortal injury."

"I'd love to see a bullfight," said Stuart. "So far all I've seen is that business where they walk down the street in New York. I hear in Greece they throw huge pottery jars from the windows to make noise."

"And what are the Waterhouse Easter traditions?" Matthew asked, expecting the pair of siblings to spout all manner of memories. Given how playful they were with each other, he had no doubt they'd given their parents a challenge as youngsters. Especially Stuart.

"Oh, our mother loved Easter," Georgia sighed. "We colored eggs, of course, and there would be a big cake and enormous meal waiting when we came home from church. She would fill the house with lilies and tell the Easter story with great dramatic flair." She nudged her brother. "Stuart gets his theatrics from Mother's side of the family."

"Peach had the luck to be born on an Easter Sunday, so some years it was a double celebration," offered Stuart, who had spent most of teatime surveying the room over Matthew's shoulder. Sizing up the social value of everyone present, Matthew surmised. It had become clear that to Stuart, life was a series of potential deals. He paid little attention to the moment because his gaze was forever fixed on the next big opportunity. Matthew was surprised he could contribute to the conversation at all, given how little notice he seemed to be paying to it.

"So you've a birthday coming up?" Matthew asked with a grin. Peach, hmm? It suited her, silly as it was.

Georgia blushed, and he could easily see where the nickname came from. She did have a peachy glow about her.

"Tomorrow!" announced Stuart. "Georgia's birthday is tomorrow."

"Stuart, hush." She swatted at him. "You shouldn't…oh dear." Her face fell as a waiter arrived to stand over Stuart's shoulder.

"Message for you, Mr. Waterhouse. At the front desk."

Georgia seemed to know how events would proceed from here. Once again, her brother was going to pull his infamous disappearing act.

"Back in a jiffy." Stuart pushed his chair away from the table. "Entertain our birthday girl for a moment, won't you, Covington?"

There was an uncomfortable silence as he buzzed off, responding to yet another important interruption. And then again, not so uncomfortable. Matthew enjoyed Georgia's company tremendously. He just wished things didn't always have the feeling of being orchestrated. He would have preferred to know she sought his company by choice, not manipulation.

Matthew stifled a sigh. It must be tiring to be so continually maneuvered by someone you love. He leaned in a bit and whispered, "I give him eight minutes before he returns to tell us he's 'dreadfully sorry but he must be going.'"

Matthew's talent at impersonations paid off, for his imitation of Stuart's voice was spot on.

Chapter Twenty-Four

Georgia gave a start, shocked at Matthew Covington's mimicry and his directness. It was one thing to know what was going on, quite another to declare it openly. For a moment it stunned her, but then she discovered it felt surprisingly refreshing. As if he respected her enough not to pretend they both didn't see what was going on in Stuart's constant disappearances.

"Mr. Covington, what a thing to say." She played for a moment at being insulted, then let a hint of her amusement show. "Personally, I'd give Stuart no more than five minutes, under the circumstances."

Mr. Covington's face creased in a gleaming smile and he pulled out his pocket watch. "Shall we see who wins?"

Georgia feigned astonishment. "Am I to understand you are suggesting a wager? Here, during tea at the Palace Hotel? The very thought."

"I'd never suggest such a thing," he replied, looking all too much as if he'd be delighted to do that very thing.

"Think of it as hypothesis and observation. A scientific study."

She shot him a doubtful glance. "A scientific study. Of Stuart's diversionary tactics?"

Her label evidently delighted him. "'Diversionary tactics.' Why, I do think that's a most appropriate term." He made a show of checking his watch. "Two minutes fifteen seconds."

"This is outrageous." She fanned herself, playing along. "I should be most insulted." But it wasn't insulting at all. As a matter of fact, it was satisfying to call Stuart at his own game.

"But you're not," Matthew retorted, "because you're far too smart for that."

"A backhanded compliment, Mr. Covington." She *was* too smart for this. Suddenly, she found herself wondering why she had ever put up with it.

He stared at her for a moment, almost indecisively. Then, after looking over her shoulder toward the hotel desk, as if to judge how much privacy they had before Stuart's return, he leaned in. "Then I shall pay you a true compliment, Miss Waterhouse. I find you a most delightful woman, honorable and admirable in every detail. And..." he softened his voice until it seemed to tingle down the back of her neck "...in possession of the most astounding eyes I believe I have ever seen."

He stared at her again, for how long she could not say. His expression confounded any attempt at words. He found her delightful. Honorable and admirable. Not just the sibling shadow of her outlandish brother, but *her.* And to think that he found her eyes astounding, when she could hardly think of words to describe *his.* Their impossibly deep indigo seemed to pin her to her chair.

His directness flustered her. He spoke as though her opinion meant something to him. And that was a rare thing indeed for the sister of Stuart Waterhouse.

After a pause that seemed endless and yet far too short, Georgia saw his gaze shift over her shoulder. "Four minutes fifty seconds," he said in a conspiratorial whisper. "You win."

On cue, Stuart appeared at her right side, a stack of papers in his hand and a waiter just behind him. "Crisis at the office. I've got to run, Covington, it can't be helped. But…" He stepped out of the way to reveal the waiter holding two slices of lemon cake, a specialty of the house, and one of Georgia's favorites. "I thought this might keep you both from missing me. Consider it an early birthday cake, Peach, from me to you. You'll see her home, of course, Covington?"

The waiter set the slices down in front of them. "Of course," replied Covington, managing to look surprised despite his earlier prediction.

"My favorite. Thank you, Stuart. I almost forgive you." The words were hollow. Stuart was trying to be nice, in his own selfish, manipulative way, but somehow a line had just been crossed. True forgiveness felt just out of her grasp at the moment.

Stuart winked. "That'll have to do." And he was gone.

Covington gave her a sympathetic look before attempting to make the best of things. "*Is* this a favorite of yours?"

"My very favorite, as a matter of fact." She straightened in her chair. "And don't worry," she added in a firm voice, "I have every intention of making Stuart bring me back here tomorrow for more. He can buy my forgiveness today, but it won't excuse his obligation tomorrow, I assure you."

"Well then, I suppose I should have to reluctantly thank Stuart for the opportunity to see you again tomorrow. Perhaps we should consider tying your brother to his chair so as to insure you an uninterrupted birthday luncheon."

Georgia imagined Stuart lashed to his chair with the red velvet stanchions from the hotel lobby. "That would be something to see," she laughed. "Then one of us would have to feed him his cake."

"I do believe I'll leave that duty to you," Mr. Covington said before taking a bite of his cake. He nodded in approval of the fluffy, lemony confection, and some part of her was pleased to know he liked it as well. "Happy birthday, Miss Waterhouse." His eyes held hers for a moment, the smile in them fading to something far more unsettling.

Her hand clutched her napkin under the table. His voice had the most extraordinary smoothness when he spoke softly. It seemed to ripple over her. "Thank you, Mr. Covington." She felt as if she gulped out the words.

"Please," he said, his voice gaining even more warmth, "call me Matthew. Even if just for today."

Matthew. She'd known since they were introduced that his name was Matthew. She'd heard the name dozens of times. Yet to hear him speak it, to hear him ask her to use it, was another thing altogether. Matthew. It suddenly sounded as smooth and lovely as his accented voice.

She took a breath, dared to look in him in the eye, and said, "Thank you, Matthew."

She didn't ask him to call her Georgia. He didn't expect her to. He was almost surprised she'd granted his request and called him Matthew. Not that he hadn't surprised himself by asking her.

That woman did things to him. Unsafe things he couldn't help and wouldn't deny. It was worth any impropriety to give her that moment of feeling special, when she'd been so repeatedly brushed off by her brother.

No, he didn't mind that she hadn't asked him to call her Georgia. He liked the secrecy of calling her that in his thoughts. *Georgia.* To him, now, she was Georgia, even when he said goodbye to her as "Miss Waterhouse."

And when he went back to his hotel room after seeing her home—and after daring to plant a light kiss on her hand when he helped her out of the carriage—he knew sleep would evade him tonight.

It did. He wandered about his room, restlessly turning a thousand thoughts over in his mind until the wee hours of the morning. There, in the sleepless darkness, Matthew pulled out his sword for the first time in weeks. It did not surprise him when he thought it whispered "Georgia" as it sliced through the air.

His father was fond of saying that Matthew frequently lost his composure. Matthew was beginning to think the heir of Covington was in very real danger of losing his heart.

Chapter Twenty-Five

I've no right, Father. I owe so much to Stuart. Without him, I could have been forced into a marriage by now simply to survive. Why has he begun to grate on me so? I've withstood his tricks for years without chafing, but now it's become so much harder. What is happening?

Georgia sat in her window seat, her arms hugging her knees, her toes tucked under the hem of her shift. She pulled her wrap tighter around her shoulders as a gust of wind rattled the bay window. Droplets of rain raced each other down the panes, joining and pooling, then splitting again in a glistening web across the glass. She traced one drop's path down the window with her finger. Spring in San Francisco was always an unpredictable affair—warm and welcoming one day, damp and dreary the next.

It seemed a fitting time for a birthday, as her life seemed to be changing pace. An agitation had stolen over her in recent weeks. She'd put it down to the excitement of the Bandit, but she was coming to realize it was far more than that. It had been coming on for months, long before the dark brooding hero of her imagination had appeared. Six months ago she'd have told anyone who asked that life was perfect just as it was. That things could go on in their present state indefinitely, and she'd consider herself supremely blessed.

She could no longer answer so firmly. Things could not go on in their present state, even if she had no idea what the alternative might be.

Where are you pulling me, Lord? Are You pulling me at all? Or am I simply straying, straining against You? I've never felt lonely before. Even when people could not understand how I was content, You've given me great contentment. Why remove it now?

Perhaps it was just the passing of another year that made her so pensive. She was, after all, turning twenty-five, and that seemed like an important year. One that invited retrospection. Perhaps in a week she'd look back on all this tumult as just an emotional response to the passing of time. After all, Stuart had been sour-faced a whole month earlier this year when he turned thirty.

An hour later, the thought still held no comfort. It was almost two in the morning, and if she didn't find a way to sleep, she would spend her birthday in a sorry state indeed. She read a psalm—the one about God knitting her together in her mother's womb—for it seemed appropriate to the day. She found herself wondering if this section was one of the ones cut from Matthew's Bible.

Matthew. How easily the name slipped into her mind now. She allowed herself to imagine him, sitting up late into the night, exploring the Bible Reverend Bauers had given him. She was sure she'd sensed some reaction in him when she'd read him the passage from Corinthians. Yet he did not seem a man of faith at all. Seeking, perhaps, but no faith had taken hold, as far as she could see. It seemed unwise to nurture any fondness for a man so ill at ease with himself. Still, that was how Reverend Bauers always said God shook a man to attention. With an unrelenting ill-ease. Was God shaking Matthew Covington? What an extraordinary thing that would be.

He would be a wonderful man of faith, she surmised, without really knowing why. It was just an instinct.

I'm quite fond of him, Father. You know that. And You know how unwise a thing that is.

Despite her self-lecture, the memory of his impulsive kiss on her hand this afternoon wedged its way into her thoughts. *He is fond of me, I think, but for such unusual, rewarding reasons. He sees me. I know You see me Father, and that You know me. But to be seen, be recognized by him in such a way, was so pleasing. Thank You for that blessing. A birthday present from You, it almost felt like.*

Matthew Covington, for all his attributes, was a most unwise prospect. She could recognize this, even if she kept rubbing the top of her palm where he'd touched her. No, she'd be wise to direct her energies into something else.

Perhaps in a week or two the contentment would return. She did, after all, have another man to consider. One who depended heavily upon her affections. Who existed by virtue of the fine imagination God had given her.

She had the Bandit, and he was a most excellent place to channel all those energies.

When would the Bandit have his birthday? Would he be the kind of man to celebrate the passing of his years, or ignore them? Yes, this was a much better place to focus her thoughts. Georgia let her head fall against the glass as she wondered. Her hero needed a birthday of his own. How to give him one? The scene came to her in an instant, as if it had dropped from heaven in complete form. It was perfect; dark and brooding, just like her hero. Tragic and yet deeply poignant. She heaved a sigh of thanks toward heaven and nearly ran to the desk, flipping open the top of her inkwell with such vigor that it sent a small shower of droplets over the page.

> "Black gloves laid a single white lily across the roughly hewn gravestone. Rain fell softly, darkening the granite with streaks that seemed to weep down its engraved face. She lay here, never to know the joy of flowers or spring—or her son—again. Each year the Bandit made his pilgrimage to the lonely site of his mother's grave, the woman who'd given her life in the granting of his."

"Easter is over this weekend, isn't it?" Stuart asked with annoyance. The eggs had been fine—charming even—but when the real-life Bandit had upped the ante to all those chickens, things got a little more complicated than Stuart would have wished. He didn't like someone trying to outdo him. Stuart wanted to have his hands on the reins. He wanted to know he could orchestrate events to his liking. He didn't much care for a loose cannon like this Bandit impersonator roaming his city unsupervised. He'd need to find him somehow, so he could keep him under control.

"Yes, sir," Oakman replied.

Stuart looked at him. "Who is this man impersonating my Bandit, anyway? Do we have any idea? Not that I want to stop him, mind you, but I want to know where to put the pressure if he goes too far."

Oakman leaned back, resting his hands across his belly. "There are loads of theories. But no one knows anything definite, that I can find."

"Keep looking."

"Oh, you can count on that, sir. I'm looking."

Stuart leaned against his desk and lowered his voice. "We're a month away. Are we ready?"

That brought Oakman to attention. "Near as I can tell. There are a few loose ends to tie up. One contact on the docks I'm not quite sure about, yet. I need to take a few steps to ensure his loyalty, but I don't think there'll be any problem."

A few steps. Stuart was relatively certain what kind of persuasion bought loyalty on the docks. It was a jungle down there, a predatory landscape if ever there was one. Which was just fine by him. He preferred the open food chain of the docks to the gilded treachery of Nob Hill any day.

"What about our friend Mr. Covington? Has he found anything?"

Oakman paused for a second, running his hands down his face. "He asked for a second set of ledgers yesterday. That worried me a bit. But I'm not sure it's a problem."

Stuart blew out an exasperated breath. Covington was presenting more of a challenge than he'd anticipated. Why couldn't the Brit just give in to his obvious infatuation with Georgia and stop being so studious? A healthy young man shouldn't be so hard to distract. Stuart checked his watch. "Well, I've got to meet Georgia for lunch. It's her birthday."

Oakman looked up. "Didn't you take her to lunch for her birthday yesterday?"

"No." Stuart shook his head, not hiding his exasperation. "Covington had us over to the Palace for tea. I gave her an early piece of birthday cake when you sent over the message to call me back."

"But you *told* me to send over the message to call you back, sir."

"I'm aware of that, Dex. She just didn't take it very well, that's all. Something's put a bee in her bonnet lately. She's all up in arms over little things. Told me in no uncertain terms last night at dinner that I was to take her back to the Palace today for her birthday, and that if I was to leave for any reason at all, heads would roll."

"Georgia? Said that?"

Stuart glared at his colleague. "She did. Emphatically. I don't know what's gotten her all riled up."

"What?" said Oakman, with the most ridiculous look on his face, "or whom?"

"But I've just *come* from cake." Georgia tried to resist as Quinn pulled her down the Grace House hallway toward the dining room.

The boy spun on his heels. "Don't you tell anyone that. This cake is *your* cake." He tugged on her sleeve. "Act happy to have it."

"But I am happy to have cake," Georgia replied, her heart warming at the boy's concern. "Just not so *much* of it."

"We *made* you this cake," he said, as if that should be argument enough. "Is icing supposed to be green?"

Georgia tried not to consider the possibilities. "Some is. Icing comes in lots of colors."

"We only got green. So pretend you like it." He seemed to consider it his job to manage her participation. *Just what I need,* she thought for a moment, *another male telling me what to do.* When she noticed a large splotch of something greenish on Quinn's elbow, she decided perhaps it was not as bad as all that.

Quinn halted in front of the closed dining room door. "Come in here for a moment, Miss Georgia," he shouted in a rehearsed tone, evidently providing the "cue" needed by those within. "We've got something to show you," he bellowed.

Quinn pushed open the door to a room filled with smiling faces. A pack of recently scrubbed, smeary-aproned "bakers" yelled "happy birthday" around a lopsided green cake. It wasn't a happy green, more brackish than lime-colored, with a frightening collection of black bits, but the cheery expressions couldn't help but make Georgia chuckle. Reverend Bauers had a "we did the best we could" expression that only deepened her laugh.

The exquisite lemon cake at the Palace Hotel might have delighted her palate, but this questionable confection delighted her heart. She clasped her hands theatrically. "My goodness," she exclaimed, "I'm absolutely surprised."

"We made it!" a small child to her left boasted, pointing

with pudgy green-tinted fingers as one corner of the top layer slid slightly off its base. "Can you tell?"

"Not at all," Georgia said. "It looks like you just brought this from the finest bakery in the city."

Reverend Bauers extracted himself from the sticky crowd and came around to pull out a chair at the head of the table. "Miss Waterhouse, will you share your cake with us and celebrate your birthday?"

"I'd be delighted."

As he pushed in the chair, the children scattered to their own seats, eager for a piece of their creation.

"There's room for one more, I trust?" Matthew Covington's voice came from behind her. "I missed the earlier birthday cake." Obviously, he'd not seen the cake in front of her, or she doubted he'd ask.

Georgia whirled to face him, giving him an exaggerated wink. "Oh, but Mr. Covington, I've had *no* cake yet today."

Chapter Twenty-Six

Matthew seemed confused. "Have you not just come from—"

Georgia raised both eyebrows, hoping to cue him to follow her lead. "No," she said, overenunciating and nodding almost imperceptibly to the crowd behind her, "I've been *hoping* for cake all day and had *none.*"

Matthew glanced at her, cast his gaze to the baked atrocity on the table, then looked back at her. She gave him her most blatant "play along" expression.

"Of course," he finally said, only barely hiding a laugh. "And here you were saying to me just yesterday how much you liked…" he chose his description carefully "…green cake. How very fortunate for you."

"Fortunate for *you,* you've come in time to join us," she said, nearly laughing at the situation. She was certain he was no more enamored with the idea of eating such a cake than she. She was also certain he'd play along in heroic proportions rather than disappoint such an endearing audience.

"Indeed," he said, his eyes darkening to mean any of a thousand things. "And how very…green…a cake it is. I *must* have a piece before Reverend Bauers and I attend to urgent business."

Did he have urgent business with Reverend Bauers? Or was that merely a strategic improvisation? He was holding something behind his back. Either way, she envied his alibi, for she had nothing more urgent than a role of uncut bandages to save her from so green a cake.

"But no business more urgent than this," he declared, producing a lovely bouquet of lilies. Delicate yellow lilies the color of lemon cake. "Since I missed our earlier…appointment. Happy birthday, Miss Waterhouse."

She took the flowers from him. Two of the older girls cooed and poked gentle fingers at the blooms. "They are delightful, Mr. Covington. Thank you so very much." As she said his full name, his request to call him otherwise echoed like a vibration through her chest. "Do sit down."

"From the look on your face—" Reverend Bauers put the book he was holding back on the shelf "—you're up to something. And I daresay it's more than providing Miss Waterhouse with a birthday bouquet."

Matthew pretended surprise. "Me? However could you say something like that?"

The clergyman leaned forward and whispered, "Oh, a recent event involving agitated chickens."

He stepped back with an elaborate bow. "Well, my good Reverend, you have me there. But poultry aside, we have a bit of work to do if a certain hero is to give another Easter gift to his fair city."

Bauers's expression grew serious. "I've given thought to that, Covington. I don't think it would be proper to do anything else near Easter. It is a holy season, and given to contemplation and sacrifice, not theatrics. I'd much rather see you at our Good Friday service than out conducting heroics. *Very* much rather."

Matthew should have known it would come to this. Sooner or later, the good reverend would try and drag him into a church service, especially at Easter. After all the man had done to aid him, did Matthew really have grounds to refuse? "I'm not at all sure," he said, stuffing his hands in his pockets, mostly because he couldn't think of a stronger retort.

"No one needs you to be sure. We just need you to be here." The clergyman raised an eyebrow. "Unless you have other plans?"

Other plans. He had no holiday plans. While he had somehow expected the Waterhouses to extend an Easter invitation, he really had no basis to expect such a thing. At the moment, it looked as if he would be spending his Easter with Thompson in his room. Or eating alone in the Palace dining room.

"Come now, Matthew," the reverend said, using his Christian name for the first time—intentionally, Matthew guessed. "Unless Stuart Waterhouse is planning to spirit you elsewhere, everyone you could call friend will be at the service here—including Miss Waterhouse. And me. And, if you must know, a couple of young men who skewered you not too long ago and have since repented."

Reverend Bauers was pulling out all stops and brooking no refusal. What had Matthew's father once said to him? *It does you no good to start a fight you can't win.* Matthew sighed. "Very well then, what time should I be here?"

Reverend Bauers clasped both of Matthew's shoulders. "I knew you'd come round."

"And how did you know that?"

With a wink, the reverend nodded toward the heavens.

Egad, thought Matthew, *that's the first time I've been in a room with one other person and been outnumbered.*

Matthew was delighted to discover Georgia was still at Grace House when he finished—if one ever truly finished—with Reverend Bauers. He'd planned to give her the flowers in relative privacy, not amidst the giggling pack of children. Still, it had been pleasant enough to catch her eye here and there in the chaotic conversation, to sneak a glimpse of her admiring the flowers as she showed them to the girls around the table. He had pleased her, and he liked that.

Which was, of course, not helpful. He must return home to England when his business was completed, and he knew in his bones that England would never suit her. Still, Matthew seemed unable to squelch the impulse to make her happy. To, when he was honest with himself, "rescue" her from the apathy of her surroundings. And that had always been Matthew's vice: rescuing even when no rescue was needed.

Even if it meant ingesting the strangest concoction to ever be called "cake." As he recalled the green-gray dessert they'd shared, he wondered if Georgia's stomach had turned over as many times in the last hour as his had. She did look a little peaked when he found her putting away the last of the bandages in the storeroom. It did not escape his notice that the lilies lay on the table beside her.

"Have you fully recovered from your party?" he asked as he leaned in the storeroom doorway.

She gave a lopsided grin and put her hand to her stomach. "I'm not quite sure. They did a most…enthusiastic…job, didn't they? I'm worried that our poor cook may never recover from the experience."

Endearing. That was the word he'd give to her expression. She looked so full of affection for this place and these people that she'd gladly have swallowed frogs. For the first time he admitted to himself how envious he was of that affection. "I'm worried myself," he said, trying not to wonder if she would put her tender hand to his forehead if he pleaded ill. "I hope you won't be offended if I admit to preferring the cake at the Palace."

"No," she said with a laugh. "Not at all."

Matthew came into the room and nodded at the bandages. "Still working? Haven't you celebrations to attend to? Ones involving *actual food?*" He regretted the question the moment it left his lips. What if she had no celebrations planned? What if lunch with Stuart was the most she received on her birthday? It stung him that he'd asked so pointed a question without thinking.

"I'll have a lovely dinner with my brother. Cook always makes my favorites. And I have many plans for Easter to pull together, so I'll be quite busy."

Matthew wondered if being born on Easter wasn't really the blessing Stuart made it out to be. The feast moved every year, sliding in and out of the path of Georgia's birthday, it was true. But to Matthew it seemed Easter was yet another force determined to overshadow this extraordinary woman. His own mother spent days elaborately celebrating her birthday—and demanding others do the same. Did everyone brush aside Georgia's birthday because it fell too near to Easter? Did she do anything other than pause for a few slices of cake before resuming rolling bandages and seeing to her household? She deserved better.

He decided on a birthday present of another kind. "Bauers's convinced me to come back Friday. I thought you'd like to know."

She blinked at him for a moment before she registered his meaning. When she did, she put down the bandages and turned to face him fully. "For Good Friday services? Oh, yes, Matthew, I am delighted to know."

She had called him Matthew without thinking about it. Her immediate blush told him so. Which meant that she had been using that name in her thoughts. Which meant she had been thinking about him. A jolt went through him.

"The service is beautiful here," she said too quickly, as if to cover up the admission, "and quite different from what I imagine you're used to. I always find it a very moving experience." Her gaze dropped back to the bandages. "I've always wanted Stuart to come, but have never been able to convince him. I'm so glad Reverend Bauers has had more success with you."

She was oblivious of her own strength. She saw Stuart's refusal as a reflection on her, instead of his own stubborn nature. Was she unaware that the prospect of seeing her again was half the reason Matthew had consented to Reverend Bauers's persuasion? Was she so blind to her qualities that these people at Grace House celebrated? Instead, focusing on the many who dismissed her? How was it she held such calm inner strength without even realizing it? How did she persevere in the face of a world that seemed to pay her so little attention?

He realized he was staring at her.

He realized he did not want to stop, nor to hide what he was certain showed in his eyes. It was doomed, what he felt for her at that moment, what he'd been feeling for days, if not from the first. It could come to no good end for either of them. And yet he could no more hold it back than he could halt the tide that would carry him back to England.

"Stuart is a fool to decline," he said quietly. He wanted to hit himself immediately. Had she not asked from the first that they not spend time discussing her brother? Was Matthew such a coward that he could only couch his hints at affection in Stuart's actions? "I'm too glad to come and see what you hold so dear," he said with more strength. "I would consider it an honor to escort you to the service."

She knew. He saw it in her eyes. No, she wasn't unaware of her effect on him. She feared it, just as he did—perhaps far more than he did. But she knew. Even if he couldn't be certain she'd known it before now, even if she'd only suspected it when he'd kissed her hand yesterday, here, now, she *knew*. It seemed as if a cannon went off in his chest. "Please…Georgia…allow me the honor."

It was a daring assumption, to use her first name without her permission, but he seemed unable to stop himself. She startled just a little bit at his boldness, but there was much more than surprise in her eyes. There was a tiny, fragile joy, a careful pleasure, that fastened itself around his heart.

"We'll...we'll see," she stammered quietly.

It was enough for now.

Chapter Twenty-Seven

Georgia was finishing up some sewing that evening when she heard Stuart's tenor ringing through the halls.

"Oh, men of dark and dismal fate,
Forgo your cruel employ,
Have pity of my lonely state,
I am an orphan boy."

She put down her work and sighed. Of course. Well, it was her own fault. She'd thought she'd penned a poignant episode of the Bandit's adventures for the Good Friday edition. She hadn't for a moment considered that she'd now employed one of the most famous running jokes of *The Pirates of Penzance* when she'd made the Bandit an orphan. She'd given the story to Stuart when they met for her birthday lunch. An episode in which readers discover the Bandit's parents are dead, which, by definition, made him an orphan. Stuart's beloved Gilbert and Sullivan pirates never harm any orphan, and are hilariously astounded when all their victims instantly "claim" to be orphans. "An orphan boy"—how had she not seen it? She was astounded he'd waited this long to come home and tease her.

It would be a long evening, even with a fine birthday meal. From now until the episode's appearance on Friday—and perhaps for weeks thereafter—the chorus would be endlessly sung to her, Georgia had no doubt.

She heard her brother's steps coming into the parlor, accompanied by a rousing chorus, "'*For he is an orphan boy, hurrah for the orphan boy!*'" Stuart's blond head popped into the room from around the corner. "*And it sometimes is a useful thing to be an orphan boy!*'"

Georgia looked up from the mound of cloth in her lap. "Most amusing, Stuart."

"And how are you, my dear orphan sister?"

It had not struck her that she and Stuart were orphans, as well. Not that she didn't know it—especially today, her birthday. But she always thought of it in terms of Stuart's phrase "we're all we have in the world." The term "orphan" seemed so much colder, despite the fun Gilbert and Sullivan had with it.

"Did you have a nice afternoon at the Grace House after our lunch?"

"As a matter of fact, I did." She smiled at the memory of the ominously green cake. Reverend Bauers had said the most beautiful prayer over it. It had tasted more like medicine than confection, but she'd made a spectacle of herself complimenting the children for their efforts. She was only outdone by Matthew Covington, whose outlandish string of superlatives reduced everyone to laughter by the end. It was truly a delightful, if not delicious, celebration.

Her brother looked puzzled. "I still say it's an odd way to celebrate your birthday. Ripping bandages."

How wrong he could be about some things, for so smart a man! Her work at Grace House was so much more than ripping bandages. These people were as much her family as Stuart. She could think of no finer way to celebrate her life than to do the things that gave her joy. And Grace House always gave her joy. The fact that Matthew had been there had given her great joy, as well—even though it felt dangerous to admit it.

She had tried not to be disappointed when he did not appear at the Palace as she and Stuart had lunch—and more lemon cake. Instead, she had attempted to reassure herself that it was just as well not to nurture that friendship. To remind herself how foolish her growing affection was.

He felt something for her. She knew it, could feel it in how he'd looked at her when he said he was coming to Grace House on Friday.

He was coming to the church service.

He wanted to come with her. *With her.* Did he realize what that meant to her?

The lilies he had given her, now standing in a crystal vase on the parlor table, had not left her side all afternoon.

She shared none of this with Stuart.

"I enjoyed my afternoon immensely, Stuart. And so did you, from the look on your face."

Stuart swept the needlework off of her lap and pulled her to her feet. "My look has nothing to do with me. It has to do with you. With your birthday present. I've come up with the most marvelous gift for you, Peach."

Georgia often felt a mild sense of alarm when Stuart got that expression on his face. "And what is that?"

"I'm going to throw you a ball."

"A ball? For my birthday?" Georgia felt the room shift a little under her feet. It was not a pleasant sensation.

"Well, not exactly a birthday ball. It's a little late to pull something like that off on a grand enough scale."

A grand enough scale? She furrowed her brow.

"A great big ball. Isn't it a fine idea?" He didn't wait for her answer before adding, "But it's not just any ball, Peach."

"What do you mean?"

He dropped her hands and crossed his arms across his chest like a conquering major general. "I'm going to throw a Bandit Ball. I'm going to throw you a ball in a few weeks and we're going to invite the Black Bandit to show his face. You're going to meet the man who's been bringing your fantasy to life, Peach. He'll never know it's you, but you'll get to know it's him. You'll meet your Bandit. Are you pleased?"

Georgia gulped in a breath. "I don't know what I am. I don't know what to say."

Stuart pulled her into a waltz. "Say the only thing you ought to say—yes!"

"I cannot imagine where he got this wild idea to throw a Bandit Ball." Georgia pushed a cart full of reading primers as she and Sister Charlotte walked through the convent school a few days later. The convent was donating some educational materials to Grace House, and Georgia was only too glad to have another opportunity to visit Sister Charlotte. "It's a dreadful idea, don't you think?"

Charlotte selected another book from the shelf behind her and added it to the cart. "Why, not at all. I think it's a grand idea. For any number of reasons."

Georgia's spirits deflated. Was she the only person who thought this a poor idea? Did anyone care what *she* thought of a ball proposed as *her* birthday present? "And those grand reasons are?"

Charlotte pushed open a supply closet door. "First of all, you'll get to meet your Bandit under the most advantageous conditions. He has no idea of your affections for him, but because of your status as Stuart's sister he'll be bound to pay attention to you."

Charlotte still had no idea that Georgia penned the Bandit's adventures. No one knew the truth, and it was going to stay that way. If Charlotte—or anyone—merely thought her interest in the Bandit was because of Stuart, or if they persisted in their belief that Stuart was really George Towers, then that was fine with Georgia. It made things infinitely easier. "True."

"You'll get to see the man up close," she continued, selecting three more books from a narrow wooden shelf, then adding some small slates and a ceramic container of stubby pencils, "not hiding behind the costume and the legend. You have no idea how illuminating it can be to see a legendary man up close. Some of them grow more compelling the nearer they get. Others, well—" she erupted into a chuckle "—let us just say they pale under scrutiny."

Georgia took the supplies and stacked them on the cart with a dubiously raised eyebrow.

"Oh, I know of what I speak. You may find the fastest antidote to your infatuation might be spending ten minutes in close proximity to the man." Charlotte handed over the last of the books and dusted off the front of her habit. "The stories I could tell! The heroes I could bring down."

As outlandish as it sounded, it made Georgia wonder about Charlotte's late husband, Robert Brownstone. What kind of man had finally won Charlotte's heart? What had he done? How had he risen victorious over so many heroic characters?

Georgia was drawn out of her thoughts by the waving of a pencil in front of her face. "Really, dear, you must stop drifting off like that. It hides your intellect." The nun waved to a young priest coming down the hallway. "Father David, would you please see to it that these supplies are delivered to Grace House?"

"Yes, Sister." Off went priest and cart.

"Now," continued Charlotte, "back to the business at hand. You're going to invite your other man—the real-life man—to the ball, are you not?"

"Goodness. I hadn't thought about that. I don't even know if he'll still be in San Francisco." Distant shouts heralded the letting out of girls from class elsewhere in the building.

"This will give him reason to extend his visit," said Charlotte. "Have you seen him since our last conversation? Have you revised your opinion of him in any way?"

Georgia felt a blush rise in her cheeks. "As a matter of fact, I have." Carefully, without mentioning any names, places or other identifying details, she told Charlotte the story of the tea and cake and her birthday flowers.

"Matthew Covington? The man is *Matthew Covington?*"

Chapter Twenty-Eight

Georgia nearly gasped. She'd taken the greatest of care not to reveal his identity. "How did you...?" She could not even finish the sentence.

"My dear girl, this is a convent, not a deserted island. We still do get asked to events and we still do meet people. Especially visiting dignitaries. And I must say Reverend Bauers has been rather vocal about Covington's dramatic scrape over at Grace House. And then there is Stuart. He likes to make sure everyone knows he knows everyone important." One hand flew to her chest. "Really. I do wonder how you put up with that brother of yours."

It wasn't as if Georgia hadn't heard that sentiment expressed many times before. She heard that remark, or something like it, frequently. But she usually fended it off with a comment about how Stuart had a big heart, or how he loved her dearly even if he did have an odd way of showing it, or how it took a big spirit to run a big paper. Today, though, she found such responses hollow and false.

"I suppose I wonder myself," she said, surprised at her own open admission.

"You're not him, you know. You're not alike at all. You're the furthest thing from each other that could be."

It was as if Charlotte had given voice to a fear Georgia had never allowed herself to recognize. A thought she'd never articulated, never even dared to name. She was afraid that people thought her like Stuart. That people mistook her tolerance for approval. That people never saw her behind the glare of Stuart's high-energy personality. Seemingly out of nowhere, Georgia felt a lump rise in her throat. She swallowed hard, thinking it a very foolish thing indeed to grow teary in a school hallway.

Charlotte, however, was far too keen a soul not to notice the effect her words had on her companion. She grasped Georgia's arm and squeezed it affectionately. "That's part of it, isn't it, dear? To spend your life alongside someone like Stuart. You fear yourself invisible."

Invisible. It was as if Charlotte had chosen the very word Georgia couldn't bring herself to use. Is this what nuns did? Bring people to the point where words evaded them, and they could only nod?

"My dear Georgia, none of us is invisible to God. He sees all that we do. All that we bear. All we yearn for. Surely you know that in your heart?"

"I do," Georgia replied, her voice a bit shaky. "But…"

"But knowing something and feeling it are two different things, aren't they?"

Georgia nodded.

"Mr. Covington. Does he make you feel invisible?"

"Oh, no, not at all," Georgia replied, with more enthusiasm that was perhaps wise. "Quite the contrary."

"There is much to be said for that." Together they walked through a sea of girls toward the convent garden.

"There is also much to be said for the huge distance between London and San Francisco," Georgia murmured. "And for a heart of faith and a heart without faith."

Charlotte patted her hand. "Ah, now, that's a real issue. Oceans can be crossed. Households can be moved. A man's faith is not so easy a challenge. I daresay you are right to hesitate." She opened the garden gate. "Does he know of your faith?"

"I'm sure he does. We've spoken of it directly."

"Well, that's certainly promising. What did you discuss?"

Georgia's heart gave an unsettling flip as she remembered the scene in the park. "He asked me to read him my favorite scripture. I'm quite sure it affected him to hear it. I mean, I suppose I'm sure. You can never be sure about something like that, can you?"

"Nonsense," countered Charlotte. "I believe you can be."

"Still, admiration of faith, and faith of one's own, are very different." Georgia fingered a broad green leaf on a plant to her left.

"An excellent point. How would you describe Mr. Covington's faith?"

Georgia thought about it for a moment. Matthew had tried not to be affected by the scripture she had read, but she knew it had had an impact upon him. It was in his eyes even if he hadn't said so. And somehow, without their even discussing it, she knew he was struggling with whether to delve into the Bible Reverend Bauers had given him. Was God, in fact, "on his heels," as the reverend was so fond of saying? Was that why God had brought Matthew into her life? The thought seemed far-fetched, yet appealing. She felt a grin sneak across her face. "Ready to pounce?"

Charlotte sat down. "God has certainly been pouncing on unlikely men since the time of Moses." She spread her hands wide. "Why not your Mr. Covington?"

Matthew looked up from cleaning his sword when the clock chimed eleven. After a dreary dinner at the Oakmans', during which the couple seemed intent on securing themselves in his good graces by way of endless compliments, he'd retired to his room. As the son of a powerful businessman, he'd been the recipient of such attention enough times to recognize it. Still, he never could stomach it the way his father and brother could. They saw it as the necessary lubrication of the gears of commerce. To him it rang insincere.

It made him think of Georgia. How opposite they were. Here he was, under the glare of so much unwanted attention. Eyed by dozens of people who were watching to make sure he did his duty. She, on the other hand, went about duties far beyond and in many ways beneath her station without the slightest bit of recognition or notice. How could she endure the disparity, when it chafed at him so?

Matthew's gaze fell on the small Bible sitting at his desk. Did her faith gave her that steadiness he admired?

He was almost embarrassed to be considering the question, although he didn't know why. *Because you have no faith,* he told himself. *And you won't pretend you do. At least you respect God enough not to employ Him as lubricant to the gears of life.* One had to have faith to benefit from it.

He'd heard of people "coming to faith." There'd been a cousin several years back, an idealistic young man who'd left a promising post with a fine firm to go off and teach natives somewhere. So obviously, one could acquire faith, for the cousin in question had been quite the rake before God got ahold of him.

But how did one acquire it? Did you hunt it down? Or did it come upon you unbidden, like an illness?

Or love.

Was he in love with Georgia Waterhouse? Matthew mused. What a mess that would be. He was taken with her. Extremely. Dangerously. But he was not ready to use a powerful word like love. He'd try not to be, if one had a choice about such things.

Georgia's faith was an inseparable part of her. One could not admire the woman without admiring her faith. And he did admire it, greatly. He just didn't think he could go beyond admiration to the sharing of that faith. He didn't think it worked that way.

Still, Matthew owed it to Georgia not to make a pretense of the services on Friday. He would, he decided as he put the sword back into its case, make an honest attempt at participation. Out of respect for her and all the people who had been so kind to him at Grace House. And there was really only one way he could think of to do that.

He ignored the trepidation that assailed him when he walked over to the desk and picked up the Bible. He'd open it. For her. To respect her.

Since it was the fate of Jesus they would be honoring, Matthew calculated that the life of Jesus would be the story to read. Those were laid out in the four Gospels—he remembered that much from the half-dozen Sunday school lessons he'd endured. They were somewhere toward the back. He was relatively certain he'd recognize the four names when he came to them.

He laughed when he came across the first one: Matthew. Well, if one had to pick a place to start…

Chapter Twenty-Nine

Sudden chords from the small chapel piano brought Matthew's thoughts back to the service. It was a simple, honest service. Reverend Bauers read scripture passages telling the story of Jesus's trial, crucifixion and death, interspersed by half a dozen somber hymns. Had Matthew attended such a service back in England, he would have found it dour and depressing.

His own response today surprised him. The seriousness did not seem out of place anymore, for he knew the story. In fierce detail. And now those details came upon him with such intensity that they seemed to puncture him. He'd never considered the possibility of the world—the universe itself— hanging on the outcome of a single day. It wouldn't fit into the confines of human logic.

This man, this "savior," had gone to a grisly death reserved for the lowest criminals.

And he went *by choice.* That was the part that festered in Matthew's spirit. If this Jesus really had all that power, was who He claimed to be, then why this outcome? Why not go straight to the victory everyone celebrated on Easter Sunday? It made no sense. Matthew had been angry the first time he'd read the gospel last night, thinking it all unjust torture. A waste of a good man. Why would a God as powerful as that allow such a thing to become the pivotal moment in human history?

Agitated, Matthew had stayed up later to read it all a second time. He was sure he'd somehow missed a crucial element, some key point that would let the story make sense.

But the clear choice of it, the dozens of times a mighty God could have stopped it all, had not changed. There was no other conclusion: it was Jesus's conscious choice to endure this gruesome thing. This hideous mistake that was really no mistake at all, but planned from the dawn of time.

Why? Matthew's whole being seemed to resonate with the word as the readings followed the plot to destruction.

Halfway through the service, Reverend Bauers read the passage where Jesus, in the throes of pain and suffering, gave his mother to another disciple. Matthew heard a small whimper next to him and realized Georgia was crying. His heart ached for her. For her devotion, for her acceptance, when it seemed all he could do was resist.

Then—quickly or gradually, he couldn't really tell—the resistance grew too much to bear. His heart went legions beyond aching for her and her devotion, and began aching for everything. It was as if all the details crushed down upon him, breaking his heart wide-open, in a way he didn't recognize but somehow always knew existed. And he couldn't bear to resist anymore. Because he realized it wasn't the injustice he was resisting, it was the unfathomable love behind it.

This story was never about power or justice or any of the things he'd thought before. This was a love story.

The readings went on, pushing toward the terrible end, where the final hymn hung in the air like a funeral dirge and tears shone on Georgia's cheeks. For the first time, Matthew glimpsed what it was that she saw. And he felt his heart crush. Yet it wasn't an obliteration, it was a transformation. As if his heart were crushed to burst open again. Burst open to reveal an affection. Matthew thought about what he felt for her—sorry excuse for a man that he was—and realized that it must have been only a shred of what this God would have to have felt for mankind—for *him*—to endure such a gruesome path.

There was a large hill on Matthew's property when he was a boy. Legs churning, he would run toward the top until his lungs burned, toward the place where he could see the valley on the other side. He was always running so fast, and the summit was so broad, that he never quite knew when he'd hit the top. It didn't really have a top. It was more like a shift, a realization that his churning legs were now going down, and he could see the valley. The sensation that he'd shifted sides without truly knowing when it happened.

It was like that.

He believed.

It wasn't a single moment or a great, peaking precipice, but a slow shift that altered his view. The churning of all those details, all the people newly come into his life, all the feelings surging up inside of him, had propelled him toward a summit he had almost imperceptibly reached.

And now he believed.

It was both awesome and quiet at the same time. Like a rope drawn so tight it finally snapped, but then again, not at all like that. Like a gear finally slipping into place, but not at all like that, either. As if everything made sense, but now had been turned inside out.

He realized, as the events of the past few weeks strung themselves together in his mind, that God had been propelling him up the mountain even before Matthew knew it. That the path had been there all along. Reverend Bauers, Georgia, even the boy who'd cut him—these people were placed in his life, at this time, for a reason. He was the man he was, faults and strengths, for a purpose. Unique by design. Loved beyond his comprehension. Sent.

He believed.

He found himself having to tell his body to breathe in and out, for it no longer seemed to work right. Nothing had changed, and yet everything seemed in far sharper focus. He felt as if he should run and shout, but wondered if he could move at all. It may have been minutes until the end of the service, or it might have been hours; he seemed unable to tell. He stared at the edge of the pew in front of him without seeing it. How very odd to be caught by surprise by something that hadn't sneaked up on him at all. God had, just as the reverend had said, gone "after him with both barrels blazing."

And Matthew hadn't even recognized Him until Georgia Waterhouse stared so hard at God that He came into view.

Now what?

At some point the service would come to an end and he'd need to walk out of this dear little chapel and return to the world he'd known. How would it change? Would it change at all? How would the Matthew Covington of faith be different from the Matthew Covington of before? Was it visible? It seemed both worthy of shouting from rooftops and excruciatingly private at the same time. He found himself, quite simply, at a complete loss.

The service did come to an end, and the congregation followed Reverend Bauers's instructions to file out in respectful silence. The door to the church was closed with a declarative thud. Matthew felt slightly dizzy.

Out of the corner of his eye, he caught Georgia's concerned glance. "Are you well?" she said, putting a gentle hand on his elbow. The tender touch felt as if it would knock him across a room. He wanted to take her hand and cling to it, but forced himself to tuck it into his elbow with any semblance of formality he could muster.

"May we walk?" he choked out, his voice unfamiliar.

She noticed his strange tone, and stared at him for a long moment before nodding. Somehow sensing his need for silence, she led him around the building into the mission's garden. They ended up standing in the small courtyard, where he'd been cut what seemed so long ago.

He sat down on the wide rim of the fountain facing a small fruit tree just venturing to bud. Signs of newness—something he usually never noticed—seemed to surround him. Buds, sprouts, new leaves…*ugh:* He thought it all a bit conspicuous of the universe to get so metaphorical all at once.

He was not fond of poetry. Was it appropriate to hope that faith did not lead one immediately to artistic pursuits?

The sheer ridiculousness of the thought forced a laugh out of him, but it sounded far more like a sputtering cough.

Something was very wrong with Matthew. His agitation had begun somewhere during the middle of the service, and it was nearly palpable by the end. He seemed unable to talk, and yet kept growling with some kind of furor. Had he been insulted by the dark drama of the service? Had Reverend Bauers forced him to attend somehow, and angered him? He looked as though he might launch into a tirade at any moment. When his face contorted and he choked, Georgia panicked. "Goodness," she said, alarm in her voice. "Are you ill?"

He blinked at her, looking as if she'd spoken a foreign language he couldn't understand. Was he having some sort of spell? If he fell over, she'd be quite unable to stop him from toppling into the fountain. She grabbed his hand, worried that he might start swaying at any moment.

The moment she reached toward him, he clasped her hand. Hard. "Matthew," she said, as loudly as she dared, not sure he could even hear. "Gracious, what is wrong?"

He looked at her for a long moment. "I believe," he said, his voice full of surprise and concern.

It didn't make any sense. *I believe I'm going to be ill? I believe you've insulted me? I believe I'll have ham for dinner? I—*

"I believe," he repeated, clutching her hand for emphasis. "I *believe.*"

The entire world stopped and turned. Truly, it felt as if

even the trees perked up and took notice. She widened her eyes. "Matthew?"

He shook his head, pulling one hand from hers to run his fingers agitatedly through his hair. "I believe. *It.* I read through that Bible three times last night and…I believe."

He seemed so shocked, so completely taken by surprise, that she couldn't think how to respond, except maybe to cry, which seemed inappropriate but rather unavoidable. Reverend Bauers always had the most wonderful things to say to someone who'd just come to faith, but every single word seemed to desert her. She felt a tear steal down her cheek, and prayed for the right words of response. Nothing came to her. She clasped his hand more tightly.

He looked up at her, bewildered. "What do I do now?"

The response came upon her immediately, and she knew where Reverend Bauers gained his insight at such moments. Surely, only God could grant such timely wisdom.

"It is Good Friday, my dear Mr. Covington. There is nothing to be done. The greatest work has just been done for us. We need only accept it."

Chapter Thirty

Reverend Bauers clasped Matthew's arm with great enthusiasm the next morning. "My son, I could not be happier to hear what you have said." He eased himself down on the fountain rim, patting the ledge beside him in an invitation for Matthew to join him.

Matthew couldn't suppress a smile as he sat beside the old man. The reverend's rampant enthusiasm for Matthew's newfound faith was as entertaining as it was heartwarming. The man was practically giddy, exclaiming that he couldn't have been more surprised. The knowing smirk behind his smile, however, hinted that he'd suspected nothing less. In fact, he looked so satisfied that Matthew hadn't wondered if Bauers himself had been beseeching God to go after him all along. He felt as if God *had* been after him from the moment he'd set foot on American soil. Bauers laughed heartily when Matthew admitted as much to him.

"I've been waiting more than a few years for the right set of hands to receive that Bible. I won't say I wasn't surprised when God said you were him—it did seem like a bit of a long shot, if you don't mind my saying. But I've learned to trust God's vision as better than my own. He has been waiting for you, even when you could not see it. Even when *I* could not see it." The reverend folded his arms across his chest and narrowed his eyes at Matthew. "I believe God has special plans for your…how shall we say it? Your 'unique talents.'"

Matthew took the chubby hand of this man who had become so dear to him in such a short time. "You are more kind than I am talented, Reverend."

"I find myself debating whether you are going to tell Miss Waterhouse that you are the Bandit, or that you care for her. Or is it both? You do seem to be a man given to extremes."

"Reverend, I—"

Bauers waved his protest away. "Come now, do you think I cannot see it? I believe I knew it even before you did. When you brought her favorite flowers, my suspicions were only confirmed." His face grew serious. "Yesterday, I would have done my best to dissuade you. Miss Waterhouse is dear to me, and I'll not have her hurt."

"And today?" Matthew asked, still dumbfounded that Bauers knew at all. Had it been that obvious?

"And today I'll still not have her hurt, even if you now share a common faith. She's an uncommon woman. I'll not have you toying with her affections, Covington. Her heart is very tender. Don't venture where you do not mean to stay."

Matthew sighed. "That's just it, Reverend, I cannot say where I will be in a month's time. It is why I cannot declare my…affections…now."

"Then why even…" The Reverend's face darkened as

Matthew pulled a white ribbon from his pocket. "Oh, you do not mean to… Covington, can you not see the wrong in that?"

"To have the Bandit declare himself as an admirer of hers? And why not? No one seems to notice all that she does. She exists only as Stuart Waterhouse's shadow. His conscience. His keeper. I cannot give her encouragement for any kind of future. But the Bandit can pay her some attention."

"What good is that? It is a fantasy, Covington." Bauers raised his hands in the air. "Does she not deserve the admiration of a real man? Would you hand her a lie?"

"I have nothing else to give her. She would no sooner join me in England than I could cut off ties and stay here." Matthew lowered his voice. "Have you seen the way she looks when she speaks of the Bandit? She admires the hero. I wouldn't be surprised if Stuart wrote the episodes just for her."

Bauers's eyebrows knit together. "She deserves better."

Matthew stood up. "She deserves far more than I can give her."

"She deserves the truth. Not more shadows. Covington, don't."

"Bauers, you should know by now I'm not much good at doing as I am told."

The air was clear and pleasant as Matthew slipped into position Saturday night and waited.

She came out onto the terrace, pulling a shawl around her shoulders against the breeze. She looked beautiful, bathed in the splash of light that came from the French doors. Her gown and hair glowed in the blue-black, moonless night. It was like something out of a Shakespeare sonnet. He felt the urge to burst out of the bushes and declare his affections for her, to sweep her off her feet and ride into the sunset, like the fantasy she admired.

Instead, he waited until her back was to him. Then he reached into his pocket and pulled out a white ribbon tied to a small stone. In a slightly accented voice, he said, "Do not turn around, Miss Waterhouse. I mean you no harm, but you must not turn." He tossed the stone so that the white strip sailed into her view.

She gasped and gave a start, but did not turn. "Oh!" she exclaimed, pulling her shawl more tightly around her. He watched her plant her feet. "I…I shall remain where I am."

Matthew took a cautious step out of the bushes. "You think that no one sees, that no one knows the good you do, but you are wrong. I have seen. I know. You are a fine and admirable woman, Georgia Waterhouse." It was overly dramatic, but then again, this was a memory he was building, a memory to last a lifetime. If Stuart wrote such high drama to please her, then it must be high drama that she desired.

He took two more steps toward her, and with the tip of his sword he pushed the French doors closed, so that less light spilled out onto the terrace.

She heard his steps, saw the sword push the doors, and reacted. He heard her breath quicken, watched the way her body tensed. Two more steps brought him near enough. He could reach out and touch her hair, she was that close to him. He thought, as he looked at her in the moonlight, that if she turned, if he saw her eyes, there would be no hope for him.

He would surrender to the overpowering urge to embrace her, to kiss her, and be lost forever.

God above, he prayed, *do not let her turn. I am not that strong.*

Chapter Thirty-One

"Who are you?" she whispered, her voice a mixture of thrill and fear.

"An admirer," he said, wanting to say much more. He had thought of a dozen things to say, a dozen heroic, romantic things, just like the Bandit would say, but they all fled his mind in the reality of the moment.

"How did you know I wrote them?" she gasped.

What? Matthew nearly stumbled in his shock. *She wrote them?* Georgia wrote the Bandit stories?

Of course Georgia wrote them. Suddenly, it all made perfect sense. How could he not have seen that? How could he not have considered it? She wrote them. She was George Towers. It seemed almost obvious now.

It was *her* words he'd read to her—that was why she'd reacted so. Her words he'd mocked, thinking they were Stuart's ploys—and that was why it hurt her so. Her hero that he impersonated. The knowledge was so intimate, so terrifying, that he had trouble thinking clearly.

"The Bandit knows many things," he finally choked out. Such a ridiculous response. Then again, he was so stunned, he was lucky to have remembered to speak in an accent at all, much less wax eloquent under the circumstances.

She wrote them. She was George.

Leave it to Georgia Waterhouse to take his surprise for her and send it back upon himself threefold.

She wrote the Bandit.

He was at a complete loss.

"Will I ever know who you are?" she asked breathlessly.

He thought his heart would split open if he stayed a second longer. He must get out of there as fast as possible. He whispered, "God bless you, Georgia Waterhouse. Good night and good Easter," and backed away.

Stuart could not have been more surprised when Georgia told him of Matthew Covington's newfound faith.

"Covington?" Stuart sputtered over his coffee as they sat in the parlor after Easter dinner. "What have you done to him, the pair of you?"

Georgia fingered the lilies from her birthday bouquet, still brilliant and fragrant in their vase by the window. "The pair of us?"

"You and Bauers. Covington's not even an American citizen. Evangelizing the tourists, are we now?"

"God is no respecter of borders," Georgia retorted, turning to face her brother. The strength in her own voice surprised her. "He'd even take you in, should you ever come to your senses."

Stuart shook his head. "I'm thinking it's Covington who needs to come to his senses."

"Stuart," she chided. Tonight she found she could no longer endure his insults to her faith. "That's enough of that."

He looked up at her. When she stared at him, he pursed his lips and returned to his coffee without another word.

He had complied.

Normally, when Stuart went too far—which was almost always—she would swallow her feelings and silently endure. Today she stood her ground. And survived. She pulled in a deep breath of courage and pressed forward. "I've been thinking about your ball."

"*Your* ball," he corrected.

"No, it was *your* ball, Stuart. Given for me, I suppose. But I've decided to accept. I'd like you to have the ball for me, but I'd like to make a few changes."

That got her brother's complete attention.

"Such as?"

"It will be a charity ball, raising money for Grace House. The First Annual Bandit's Charity Ball. Every man who donates may come dressed as the Bandit. And you'll see to it that every man donates, won't you, Stuart?"

"A hundred Bandits? Peach, are you serious?"

She crossed her arms over her chest and went to stand before him. "Quite. It will be a sensation. You'll gain loads of press, and I'll gain enough money to ensure that Grace House never lacks for what it needs." She held out her hand. "Do we have a bargain?"

Stuart looked up. "What's gotten into you?"

"Do we have a bargain?"

He turned the idea over in his mind for a moment, looking, she was sure, for the escape clause. There wasn't one. Everyone got what they wanted in this bargain, including her. She had to admit it felt wonderful.

"I believe we do." He shook her hand.

Georgia leaned down, brought his hand to her and kissed it. "Brilliant. I'll have the list of things you need to do on your desk by tomorrow morning. How many waltzes are there in the Gilbert and Sullivan works, anyway?"

He gazed at her, mouth agape. "I don't know," he said slowly.

"Really? I was sure you would. Well, we'd best find out so we can give the list to the orchestra this week."

"Waltzes."

"Yes, Stuart, waltzes. Lots of them. They're my favorite. And red roses. Only red roses. But with white ribbons, of course. Yards and yards of white ribbons."

"Georgia," her brother said, furrowing his brow, "are you ill?"

"Not at all." She smiled back at him. "I'm just plain wonderful."

Chapter Thirty-Two

Matthew found Reverend Bauers on Grace House's front steps Monday morning, fixing the doorknob. "I need to speak with you," he said, pulling the clergyman into the mission by his elbow.

"Goodness," chuckled the reverend, who barely had enough time to put aside his tools. "Would that all my converts were so enthusiastic. But I didn't see you at Easter services."

"I had some matters to attend to." Bauers frowned, but Matthew pressed on. "Things have just become a good deal more interesting…" he lowered his voice "…in the area of my 'unique talents.'"

The reverend gave him a surprised look and ushered him into his study.

"I know the author of the Bandit episodes," Matthew declared the moment the door was shut.

"Stuart revealed himself to you? However did you accomplish that?"

Matthew sat down in one of the study chairs. "I did no such thing. Georgia told me."

The reverend settled beside him. "I'd forgotten that you were speaking to her. Tell me, does she share your feelings?"

"Bauers, *she* writes the Bandit. Georgia is George Towers."

"Georgia?" Bauers stared at him. "*Georgia?* She admitted such to you?"

"She admitted such to *him*. I believe I startled it out of her—I don't believe she planned to tell me—him."

Reverend Bauers leaned his elbows on his knees. With a heavy sigh, he dropped his head into his hand. "Covington, can you not see the terrible folly in all this?"

"Georgia writes the Bandit."

"Georgia writes the Bandit. And you have just as much as lied to her. Despite your feelings for her, of which she knows nothing. No, instead you have directed her attentions to an imaginary man who just *happens to be you*." The reverend looked up at him. "Yes, I am surprised. I had not known Georgia had such talents, nor did I suspect she held such sway over Stuart. But my surprise pales against my concern for what *you* are doing. Look, she is due here within the hour. I will arrange for you to be uninterrupted in the garden. Tell her, son, and do the right thing."

"I cannot."

"You could, but you will not." Bauers stood up. "You would if you really cared for her at all."

A storm brewed in the back of Matthew's throat. "I care too much for her. I care *too much* to encourage her where there is no future."

"After all you have seen this past week, how can you say

that? Who knows what God has planned? And yet you would deceive her into caring for an illusion?" The clergyman pointed a finger at him. "You have poached off her imagination, that's what you have done. Can you live with that?"

Matthew would never have believed he'd need to quash the urge to punch a member of the clergy. He'd chosen an unorthodox path with Georgia, he was well aware of that. But it was his choice to make. He could not share his future with Georgia. He would not wrench her away from her home. Was the Bandit's visit deceit? Of course it was, and some part of him ached for what he had done. But it was overthrown by his ache to be near her. For that gasp she'd made when she understood the Bandit was behind her. Matthew hadn't even realized how much until that moment. But it could not be. "Now look here, Bauers…" he growled.

A knock hushed him. "Gentlemen?" Georgia's voice called from behind the study door. "Reverend Bauers?"

Bauers opened the door.

"I heard voices raised," she continued, stepping into the room. "You two arguing? What on earth could bring you to that?"

"We were…debating a course of action," the reverend said, throwing a cold glare at Matthew.

She tugged on the ribbon that held her hat, and took it off. "Who won?"

"It is as of yet undetermined," Matthew said tersely.

Matthew watched her face. He could practically read her decision to move forward despite whatever it was she thought she'd interrupted. There was a fascinating new boldness to her features. "Well, then," she said, walking farther into the study, "I shall be happy to provide a very large and pleasant diversion."

"And what would that be?" Reverend Bauers asked.

"Stuart is throwing a ball. A Bandit Ball, later this month. And I've convinced him to make it a charity event to support Grace House."

"A Bandit Ball?" Matthew repeated, the storm in his throat turning to a great lump. "This month?"

"Two weeks from Saturday. Every man who donates can come dressed as the Black Bandit. It is at once publicity, philanthropy and a chance for our newfound hero to show himself among a bevy of admirers."

"What an extraordinary idea," Reverend Bauers said, the strain in his voice almost hidden. "Miss Waterhouse, you and your brother outdo yourselves."

"It is mostly Stuart," she said. "But in this case I am delighted to help matters along."

Lord, Heavenly Father, what have I done? Matthew wondered if God had not shown up in his life at precisely the right moment. Or precisely the wrong one. "Most extraordinary," he said, at a loss for any other reply.

"Mr. Covington, please tell me you will be able to attend."

It's not as if I'll need to find a costume, Matthew thought absurdly. "I can think of nothing more intriguing." And to think he'd found sedating chickens complicated a mere week ago.

"The door! I just remembered I left my tools on the front steps. Covington, would you mind helping Miss Waterhouse transport a few boxes of material down the street to the convent storeroom? I had hoped to help her myself, but…" Bauers gave a poorly rehearsed shrug and bolted from the study.

Matthew shook his head after the less-than-subtle departure.

"You and I seem to have an odd, flight-inducing effect on people," Georgia said with a lopsided smile. "But I am glad for the chance to talk with you. Tell me, how are you? I can remember believing from my earliest years, but in some ways I envy the man or woman who comes to faith in the full awareness of adulthood. It must be an incredible experience." She gazed at Matthew. "You looked as if someone had lit a firecracker inside you Friday night."

An apt metaphor. But more like a dozen explosives. "I can't say I've sorted it out yet. Some things feel settled, others feel completely jumbled. I'm still the same man, and yet I'm not." He knew it was unsafe territory, and yet he could not resist. "And how are you? How was your Easter?"

She did not reply right away, but instead headed down the mission hallway. "I must confess I was feeling despondent of late." She glanced at Matthew for a moment. "It is not always pleasant to be the 'other Waterhouse.' One feels small and unnoticed every now and then."

I could never ignore you, Matthew thought, but said nothing.

"Several things on Easter drove me to a long time of prayer. I'll not tire you with what they were. But I was reminded of all the souls who worked in obscurity, keeping their eye on God. Whom He sees. Sister Charlotte calls it 'the audience of One.' I've come to understand her now. It's given me a strength of sorts, I suppose." Georgia shook her head. "My goodness, I think I've rambled on, when you were so kind to ask. But it has been important to me, this awareness—oh, that's not the word. But I—I'm not making any sense, am I?"

Matthew felt a pang of remorse. Here he was, thinking he could craft an affirmation for her. She, in her wisdom, had gone looking for affirmation in the place where it truly mattered. How he flattered himself to think *he'd* brought that strength to her step. How God must laugh at his idiocies today. Matthew stared at her, thinking her so far above him that he could never hope to reach her level.

"What you must think of me." She blushed.

You have no idea, Matthew mused.

Chapter Thirty-Three

Georgia was beyond distracted for the next week. The situation seemed to have gained momentum of its own accord. The Bandit had a voice now, and she could hear it when he spoke in her dialogue. How easily she could picture the tale Quinn had first told her. Had it truly happened? Had she not invented the Bandit, not crafted the legend, but merely stumbled onto it? Suddenly everything was twisting back on itself. There seemed only one way to untangle the mess: to see him again. To know who he was. And so the ball became her best opportunity. Stuart's manipulation would be turned to her own design.

That night, Georgia gave up the struggle to write a Bandit episode and wrote an open letter instead.

"To our Black Bandit:

You defend those who cannot defend themselves. You champion the cause of the oppressed and the victimized. You move among us, masked by moonlight, unseen yet not unknown. Unmet yet not unadmired. We wish to honor you. Stuart Waterhouse hosts a ball in your honor on next Saturday evening. Many men will come in your guise so that you may circulate without revealing your identity, if you so choose. Each will make charitable gifts for the honor of donning your costume. Come and let a city show you its respect, and remind us that each man can share in your calling.

Until April 26, I remain your humble servant, George Towers. After that night, I hope many will have the honor of calling you friend."

If Stuart resisted running the installment, well, she'd just have to find a way to convince him. But *oh, Lord, could you grant me another visit from him? Would that be too much to ask?*

Matthew waited in the terrace shadows even though he shouldn't have.

He knew he shouldn't.

God probably had tired of telling him that.

He waited anyway. He knew Stuart was out tonight—he'd been invited to the same dinner himself—and Georgia was most certainly alone. She would come. Even if the note he'd secretly sent her earlier today had asked her to travel miles in the middle of the night, she would come. A corner of his mind wondered if she would go to such lengths for Matthew Covington instead of the Bandit but he hushed his thoughts.

The latch on the French doors clicked and Georgia stepped out onto the terrace. She had dressed in darker tones tonight, a smartly cut dress with only a small bustle, in an indigo that matched the night, and a mesmerizing cascade of small pearl buttons that looked like stars against the night sky. The shade emphasized the luminous quality of her skin, and made her beauty seem that much more ethereal. Had she dressed for the meeting? Did she realize how beautiful she was, how fragile she looked standing there clutching her wrap about her shoulders?

"Are you there?" she called in a voice just above a whisper.

"Yes," he replied from his place in the shadows, almost forgetting to alter his voice. She looked in his direction and he backed farther into the darkness.

"Why do you alter your voice?" she asked.

He paused a long time, struggling for an answer. "It is for the best." He knew she expected him to drop the pretense when she identified it, but he did not. He could not.

"Do I know you by day?" Her voice revealed a hint of frustration. Matthew realized she was probably insulted that he retained his secret once she had disclosed hers. Had she assumed that was why he had called again? In order to show his face?

"That is not a safe question to answer," Matthew replied, admiring her persistence.

She crushed a bit of her skirt in one delicate fist. "I wish to know who you are."

"That cannot be."

"Now or always?" she pressed. Georgia took a half step toward him, forcing him to retreat farther into the bushes. She was disappointed, and it was his doing. Yet he found himself helpless to stop it. He had come for no nobler reason than the driving need to see her again. To hear the catch in her voice when she spoke to the Bandit, to note the look in her eyes when she strained to see him.

"Did I create you? Or was it you that night saving Quinn from those thugs trying to steal his money?"

How on earth should he answer that? "Both," he said, opting for the strange truth.

Georgia put her hands to her forehead. "I cannot do this anymore. George Towers is a lie."

He would not have her doubt her gifts because of his cowardice. "George Towers is an act of God. Can you not see that? Can you not see the role you've been given? The gifts you have to carry it out?"

"No," she replied in almost a gasp, "I cannot. It started out as a good idea, a lark, but now… No, I thought I could see that once, but not now."

"I can. I am what you made me."

"You are more than that."

He did not answer.

"I want to know who you are. Why can you not tell me?"

Tell her, part of him cried out, his chest feeling as though it were breaking open.

You cannot. If you go to her, you will not be able to leave her, and you must *leave her. England will not disappear. Your duty will not evaporate simply because you are in love.*

And he *was* in love. For all the good it did him. The Bandit could love and be loved—even if from afar—but Matthew Covington would be prisoner to sums and tallies and England.

He turned away and ducked through the bushes.

Reverend Bauers had said the world made more sense to a man of faith. Matthew found he could not agree.

For the next few days, Matthew buried himself in the part of his life that ought to make sense. He tried to lose himself in the orderly procession of numbers, in the sheer volume of ledgers at Covington Enterprises.

The ledgers refused him any solace. Subtle discrepancies kept peeking out at him. Strange transactions. Odd numbers that seemed to fit entirely too easily into gaps created by other commerce. Produce bought too far out of season. Ships that returned to docks slightly before their voyages should have been over. Payrolls that seemed a tad too large for one ship, too small for another. Yet everything still added up—*if* one didn't look too closely. It was as if someone was poring through the books ahead of him, shifting figures, covering tracks, smoothing over clues.

"Mr. Covington, a moment?"

"Oakman." Matthew pulled his head up and rubbed his eyes.

"Everything in order, sir?"

"Yes." That wasn't a lie. Everything was in order. It was just in the wrong order, or too perfect an order… Matthew couldn't quite put his finger on it, but something in the books did not feel right to him at all. They felt tampered with, although by whom and to what end he could not yet say.

"Mrs. Oakman and I were wondering if you wouldn't care to join us for dinner tonight. Caroline says she is sure you must be tiring of hotel fare."

Matthew had planned to spend the evening going over

more documents, but he did have to admit his eyes were bleary. And sleep? Sleep had become a luxury. Some nights he hadn't slept at all. On the one hand, such wakefulness offered him great chances to pore through the tattered little Bible, and he'd learned much. On the other hand, he was becoming a bit unsteady during the day. He couldn't be entirely sure that the dark doubts his mind produced were more the product of too little sleep than of suspicious bookkeeping. Matthew was long past weary. Perhaps a good sound meal was just what he needed. Besides, conversation with Oakman could only help to shed light on things—provided he asked the correct discreet questions.

"Mrs. Oakman is quite right. I should be delighted to attend. Do thank her for me."

Chapter Thirty-Four

She was there.

It was both a wonderful and an awful turn of events to find Georgia Waterhouse and Sister Charlotte waiting with Mrs. Oakman in the parlor when Matthew and Dexter arrived at the house. Without Stuart. At first glance, Matthew thought it best to plead fatigue and end the evening as quickly as courtesy would allow. With his wits fraying, it would be the wisest thing to do.

Propriety told him he couldn't, but he knew the real reason.

The Oakmans' daughter also played the harp, and Mr. and Mrs. Oakman had invited them all into the library after dinner to hear her play. As they walked down the hall, Matthew inquired how things were going at Grace House.

"Quinn has asked Reverend Bauers for fencing lessons," Georgia reported.

"Fencing lessons?" Matthew nearly stumbled as he entered the room.

"Evidently the combination of your victory over Ian and

Michael, combined with a fascination for Black Bandit stories, has sparked an interest in swordplay. The reverend is understandably concerned."

"Ian and Michael?"

"Oh, you know them." She smiled and touched his once-injured arm. It was a light touch, yet his entire body felt the contact. "You owe your new scar to Ian."

Matthew frowned. "In my opinion, I owe my new scar to Reverend Bauers's medical skills."

"He has a good heart," she said, lowering her voice to a whisper as Amelia Oakman took her place behind the harp.

"Would that his hand were as steady," Matthew couldn't help adding, even though he had to lean close to her to do it. She smelled of lavender and something creamy that made his head swim. He saw the momentary reaction in her shoulders, the start she gave at his nearness, the smile that lingered at the corner of her mouth when she turned her attention to the music.

He, however, could not turn his attention to the music. He faced in that direction, gave the appearance of attending to the performance, but it was all pretense. Matthew watched Georgia instead.

"I've not yet heard *you* play, Miss Waterhouse," Matthew said when the girl had finished. "Stuart tells me you are quite accomplished."

"Georgia is exquisite at the harp, Mr. Covington," Sister Charlotte declared. "A gifted musician, believe me."

"As is Amelia," Georgia added. "I see great talent in you, my dear."

"Thank you." Amelia dipped into a curtsy. "Would you like to play my harp?" Amelia asked. "I should love to hear you."

"As would I," agreed Sister Charlotte.

"And I," said Matthew.

She resisted once, but finally agreed to play, and settled herself behind the instrument. Matthew was not prepared for what he saw.

Georgia was an altogether different woman when she played. Passionate. Dramatic. Matthew watched her shoulders press into the falling notes, pull others out of the velvety depth. That spark that always hid within her eyes burst into flame when she played the harp. Everything he had suspected of Georgia, everything that made her capable of writing the Bandit, emerged. She caught his eye once and he thought his heart would stop.

As they entered the carriage to ride home, Georgia wondered if inviting Sister Charlotte had been wise. She'd appeared as if she were enjoying herself earlier in the evening, but as the night wore on the nun began to look more and more agitated. Once inside the carriage, Sister Charlotte planted herself across from Georgia and crossed her arms sharply.

"Georgia Waterhouse," she said the moment the carriage lurched into motion, "I never thought I'd have cause to say this, but you are a fool." Those violet eyes gave her a look that likely stopped any misbehaving student dead in her tracks.

"A fool?"

Her slim fingers drummed against the black sleeves of her habit. "Do not think I've missed it. I have seen you back off from our young Mr. Covington because of this…this…character. The Bandit is not real. Covington is, and he is more than taken with you."

Georgia pushed out a breath. She did not wish to get into this just now. Her brain was atumble enough as it was. "Charlotte, you know he visited me. The Bandit *is* real. Mr. Covington and I can have no future, however pleasing he may be."

Charlotte untangled her arms. "I believe there is a man *portraying* your Bandit. He may be real. The Bandit is not. I wonder, Georgia, if you know the difference."

"Of course I do," she retorted.

Now it was Charlotte's turn to look exasperated. "Are you sure? Forget the Bandit mess for a moment. Covington. Can you not see how he looks at you? Has he not given you any encouragement in the matter?"

Georgia sighed. "Yes and no. It is a jumble in my head." She let her head fall against the carriage window. "Yes, he has been kind. Attentive, even." She looked at her friend. "But Charlotte, what does any of that matter if he is going back to England?"

Charlotte rose off her seat and came to sit on the cushion next to Georgia. "What does any of England matter if there is a chance for love?" She looked intently into her eyes. "Tell me. Is there a chance you can love this man?"

Georgia thought of the lemon cake, and the flowers, and the way he'd looked at her tonight. She thought of what she'd seen in the mission garden, and how he made her laugh so many times. Yes, of course she could love this man. Part of her already did. She just refused to admit it. "I cannot go to England," she said, in an almost whimpering tone.

Charlotte's voice grew tender. "And why not? What is it that you think is keeping you here? Certainly not Stuart. Bauers will be sorry to lose you, but far more eager to see you happy." She reached out and clasped Georgia's arm. "You think you cannot be happy anywhere but here, but I think you haven't even begun to know what your *own* life is. How happy you could be."

Her expression darkened. "Or perhaps it is something deeper. It is far safer to love a man who does not exist, isn't it? One who cannot hurt you because he isn't real? After all, I did say how much some real men pale under scrutiny, didn't I? Oh, Georgia, don't listen to my foolish words."

The carriage pulled to a stop outside of the convent. "I cannot tell you what to do," Charlotte continued. "That job belongs to God. But I can tell you to heed your heart. God has your own life prepared for you, Georgia. Don't miss it by staring at dreams and surrendering to obstacles."

Later that night, Matthew reread the open letter "George" had written to the Bandit. The intensity of the plea, the need he saw in it for Georgia to meet her Bandit, took down the last of his resistance.

She had to know. He wouldn't lie any longer, even if it cost him everything to reveal himself to her. She deserved no less.

She deserved so much more.

He would have to trust God with the consequences of that truth if he were to trust God at all. Even if all they would have would be the time before England called him home, who was he to say that would not be enough for her?

But how? Where? Part of him wanted to climb up her balustrade like Romeo and profess his identity tonight. An hour from now suddenly seemed too long. Then again, that moment of revelation might be all they would have. After all his cowardice, he owed her a dramatic, romantic, Bandit-worthy revelation. Perhaps it was time for Matthew Covington to write a Bandit episode of his own. And the upcoming Bandit Ball seemed ideal. Providential, even.

He found himself staring at the newspaper as if it could link him to her. *I love you,* his mind shouted into the night as he pulled on his coat. *I am the Bandit, and I love you. And at the ball, you will know.*

Chapter Thirty-Five

Matthew banged on the Grace House door until someone let him in. He demanded to see Reverend Bauers and, no, he didn't care about the hour.

Bauers eased himself down into one of the chairs after letting Matthew into his study. "I'd offer you some coffee—" he yawned "—but you don't look as if you'd care to wait that long." He ran his hands down his face and squinted at Matthew. "What is it, son?"

"I love her. She needs to know everything. I see that now."

The reverend's smile was warm despite his chiding tone. "Could you not have come to this life-altering conclusion at a more decent hour?"

Matthew simply sighed.

"Of course not. Such things seem always to hit us in the middle of the night. And you, we know, are at your best by moonlight. I have gotten far less sleep since meeting you, my friend. And I didn't get much sleep before."

"You were right. It is as much as lying to her. She deserves the truth, and she deserves to know how I feel about her, no matter where it leads." Matthew shook his head. "I sound like an idiot. Talking in valentines. I don't know what's come over me."

"Love and faith in a single fortnight? It's a wonder you're still standing. A little high-minded speech can only be expected." The clergyman settled back in his chair. "How did you come to realize this? No, wait, don't tell me. I don't want the details—there's enough of it on your face. I wish love and our Lord kept more sensible hours." He yawned again, but grinned all the same. "You're going to tell her."

"At the ball."

Bauers cocked an eyebrow. "You couldn't think of someplace more private?"

"Don't you see? It will be private. I'll be hiding among a sea of Bandits. It won't have to be a rushed meeting in the middle of the night. I can be both men at once."

"May I remind you that you *always* have been both men at once? It is only *you* who've chosen to hide one side or the other." He gave Matthew a long stare. "She shares your feelings?"

Now, here was the sticky wicket. Matthew got up from the chair and paced the room. "She cares for the Bandit. I know that much."

"Matthew," Bauers replied, "do not do this only because you think it will gain you Georgia. Do it because it is the truth, and because you know she deserves as much. Do not think to trick the lady's heart." He rested his hands on the arms of the chair. "She may be angered by your deception. Have you thought of that? You told me yourself she asked the Bandit to reveal himself, and you denied her. If she does not care for you the way you think she does, she may use the truth to hurt you."

Matthew paced the floor for a moment, hands stuffed in his pockets, considering all the possible outcomes. He stopped and turned. "It comes down to one question, doesn't it, Bauers?"

"And what is that?"

"Is she worth everything?"

Matthew could not remember being more unsettled for a social occasion. Sensing his nerves, Thompson paid extra attention to his attire. Some of that, of course, may have been the personal pride of finally getting the opportunity to show off the Bandit's costume. He fussed and fidgeted until Matthew could barely endure the attention.

As he left for the ball, Matthew had the distinct impression that he had best return with a list of compliments on his attire. And whether or not he had the best Bandit costume, he would tell Thompson that had been the case. It could not be considered lying, for how could it not be the best Bandit costume, since it was the genuine thing?

He had the head-spinning, contradictory sensation of being a public secret. The room would be filled with men pretending to be the Bandit. He actually *was,* and yet no one would know. No one but him knew that the gray shirt had been patched in one sleeve thanks to a scrape from the chicken crates. Casual observers would miss the nick in his broad black hat made by Trivolatti's meat hook. And no one, not even Thompson, knew about the odd but dear little Bible tucked under the shirt over his heart.

The absurdity of the whole evening struck Matthew as he walked out of the Palace Hotel in plain sight, dressed as the Bandit right down to the whip and a pocketful of white ribbons.

And was promptly greeted by two more Bandits.

There was no doubt this would be one of the more extraordinary evenings of his life.

Knowing Stuart as he did, Matthew thought he was prepared for the extravagance that would be the Waterhouse mansion. Despite his wildest imaginings on the subject, he found he had vastly underestimated Stuart's gift for excess. It was rather hard to find the monstrous house under all the flowers and ribbons. White bunting, festooned with billows of silver-gray fabric, strung itself around the fence like cake frosting. Where the fabric paused, cascades of flowers erupted.

Every conceivable combination of the Bandit's black trousers, dark gray shirt, black hat and gray mask wandered the grounds. The efforts at mock weaponry made Matthew chuckle; some men sported riding crops instead of bullwhips, and more than a few, rusty swords that looked as if they'd been recently wrenched off living room walls. Matthew could never describe this experience to anyone who hadn't been there.

But he couldn't merely stand and gawk; there was work to be done. He had a list of people to find and engage in conversation. A few carefully placed questions, to tongues loosened with frivolity, could provide all kinds of useful information. Matthew knew that under the right circumstances, men could be induced to boast of their crimes rather than cover them. Tonight, he guessed, plied with both drink and disguise, men might leak legions as to what was truly going on on San Francisco's docks.

Even so, tonight was really only about one conversation: with Georgia.

What would come of it, he couldn't begin to say. Would they have weeks together, then feel both of their hearts break as he lugged himself back to England? Would he uncover calamities at Covington Enterprises that would keep him here for years? Was there a way he could simply decide to stay? Tonight would certainly be easier if he had answers to these questions, but there were no answers to be had.

If any set of circumstances could drive a man to prayer, it'd be these, Matthew thought, remembering the hour he'd spent pouring his heart and his anxieties to God earlier today. *Father, guide me. This is all so new. I'm so far from home, from who I was. I'm trusting You have a plan in place.*

Matthew kept up a steady stream of prayer as he wandered from room to room, from Bandit to Bandit, working his way through his list of sources. He had failed to find Georgia after a good half an hour of mingling. Nor, he realized, had he seen Stuart.

Five interviews and three frighteningly enthusiastic Bandits later, he saw her. He had expected his heart to skip when he saw her. He had not expected the whole world to grind to a stop. She did not see him at first—proof of God's grace, he decided—for it took him long moments to recover his composure.

She wore white. A simple, exquisitely cut gown of the most iridescent, liquid white he had ever seen. It stood out among the riot of gown colors and black-gray Bandit costumes. Her hair was done up with a shower of tiny yellow flowers. She wore gloves of the palest yellow, matching the ribbon trim of her dress. Around one wrist, tied in a simple bow, was a long white ribbon. It danced and fluttered as she gestured, and Matthew felt its movement beneath his skin. If there was any question that he found her the most beautiful woman God had ever created, it was put to rest now. His admiration, his affection went far deeper than her charm or grace. It was the knowledge that inside this tiny, frail-looking creature beat a heart of courage. A soul of endurance, a warrior who wielded any weapon she could against the sins of her city. A woman so busy looking to the needs of others that she could not even see her own strength.

I would change that, he thought. *I would help her see all that she is. Remind her of all the strengths she has. I would love her, even if it cannot be forever.*

And then, as she turned and caught his eye, he added, *God help me if it cannot be forever.*

Chapter Thirty-Six

She would know him.

She wasn't sure how, but the Bandit would come and she would know it was him. The knowledge steadied her steps as she descended the grand stairway into the crowd of Bandits and other revelers. *He is here and I will find him.*

Stuart made a grandiose speech, but she didn't hear a word of it. She was scanning the room, looking at the men, wondering which one had the deep, smooth voice from her terrace. Looking at the hands, wondering which ones held the whip and the sword.

She danced with many of them, thinking that would provide the opportunity for him to reveal his identity. It proved a tiresome task—for she grew impatient with each dance, as it took only moments for her to decide this man could not be her Bandit.

Her Bandit. She'd come to think of him that way, even though it was unwise to do so. Sister Charlotte's words had pounded in her head all day—how she should look to the men in her real world and not dismiss them for a man of her imagination. It made perfect sense. It was sage advice. Georgia's heart simply refused to comply. *Once I see him,* she thought, *once I know who he is, perhaps I can settle my heart on someone else.*

She knew that for the lie it was.

There was a moment, though, where her heart skipped. She walked into the front hallway with Mrs. Oakman and caught sight of a tall man. "My dear Miss Waterhouse," he said, as his blue-black eyes danced from behind the oddly fashioned gray mask he wore. She knew at once from his accent that it was Matthew Covington. "You are the most beautiful woman in the room tonight." He took her hand and kissed it, just as he had on her birthday, and the same spark danced up her arm.

She had hoped he would come. He had dressed as the Bandit, too, which charmed her, for she wasn't sure he would. He had made the best he could as a visitor, and he had crafted a slightly tattered but very authentic-looking costume. His trousers had so many odd pockets they looked almost military, and one sleeve sported a patch. The whip coiled at his waist certainly looked far more dangerous than any of the ones carried by other "Bandits"—heaven knows where he had been forced to shop to have ended up with one so large and fierce. Other Bandits looked dashing and pirate-like. Covington looked hard-edged and, well, a bit ragged. He was the only Bandit with both whip and sword. She could not deny that the overall effect was rather eye-catching. He was somehow all the more handsome for his rough-hewn attire. Truly, if any man could come close to what she felt the Bandit ought to be, it was Matthew. Given time, the two of them could have had something.

But England would call him home soon, and so it was wise to ignore the tug she felt in her heart when he took off his hat and bowed deeply, saying, "You look stunning."

She smiled. "I see you have not quite yet fetched back your reserve."

"Tonight," he said as he gestured around the ornate hall, "seems to be a night for excess rather than reserve."

"I do not believe there is a white ribbon left in San Francisco," she mused.

"I've a few in my pocket, but I am saving them for later." He offered no further explanation when she raised her eyebrow at the comment. The orchestra started up a waltz. "I recall you are especially fond of waltzes. May I have this dance?"

"Yes." It delighted her that he remembered. "I would like that very much."

He danced well, sweeping her around the crowded floor with a fluid ease. His gaze blotted every detail out of the room until it felt as if the two of them were alone together. Which in some ways was true, for few could tell one of her Bandit partners from another for any given dance. It was a delightfully public sort of privacy.

"Bauers will be busting his buttons. You've surely raised enormous funds for Grace House."

Did he pull her half an inch closer as they rounded that turn, or did she just imagine it? "I am sorry he missed it. He'd have enjoyed it, don't you think?"

"I'm certain." Matthew continued to stare at her, hard and deliberate, as if memorizing her features. "Is it a hectic evening for you?" he inquired, and Georgia had the odd sense that it was not the question he'd intended to ask at all.

"Not as much as one would think. Stuart knows how to get things done. The decorations, I'm afraid, are all his. I was able to wrest away some control of the other parts of the evening. I must say it took him a bit to adjust to my telling him what I wanted. You can imagine it usually goes the other way around."

Matthew grinned. "So, are you enjoying your ball?"

"It is a most extraordinary evening," she said, finding every other description too complex.

"Miss Waterhouse—"

"Please!" She interrupted on an impulse, realizing she and Matthew might never have such an occasion again. "Call me Georgia. Just for tonight."

His eyes did something she could not name, something that lit up the air between them. He let his face come near to her shoulder as he pulled her into a sweeping turn. "Georgia," he said softly, and the tone of his voice nearly made her miss a step. "Georgia, I would—"

"Peach! We've got to make an announcement of how much money has been raised. Come." Stuart snatched her efficiently from the dance floor before Matthew could say a word in protest. She was beginning to despise her brother's gift for interruption.

"Thank you all for your generosity. The funds you've donated will help so many families and improve so many lives. Tonight, you are all heroes."

Georgia stepped down off the grand staircase and

accepted the congratulations of several friends. How satisfying it was to have finally redirected one of Stuart's schemes to a higher purpose. To have asserted herself at last. Months ago, she would have quietly but miserably endured the ball as Stuart's misguided idea of a gift. Now, by standing up for what she valued, she had managed to turn affairs to something that truly pleased her. And, she hoped, pleased God.

God had granted to her the one thing she most valued in her hero: courage. The most important kind—the courage to stand up for what was right. God had honored that courage, for Georgia knew that it was the first and only time many of these people had ever given money to Grace House. San Francisco was already famous for its vice. Perhaps now it could also be known for the virtue of philanthropy. She was, after all, a legendary—and now courageous—optimist.

One of the house staff approached her. "This came for you," the girl said, handing her a message. Georgia's heart stopped when she saw the rolled paper was tied with a simple strip of white cloth. She ducked into an alcove and pulled at the ribbon with shaking hands.

"George"ia—
Terrace eleven o'clock
—BB

It was him. It had to be him. Only he and Stuart knew she was George Towers. He had come, just as she knew he would. She rushed to the library to check the clock. Ten-fifty. Ten minutes! It would seem like ten years.

Foolishly, she checked her hair in the glass of the clock face. If she went through the back hallway and the kitchen, she could slip through the dining room to the terrace without having to see anyone. Georgia was quite sure she could not converse with a single soul at present. She was feeling light-headed as it was. It was best to just go now and wait on the terrace—praying the entire time, she decided.

Oh, Father, thank You. I'll accept whatever comes of this, but thank You!

Matthew was pacing the terrace like a schoolboy. He'd planned this a dozen times in his head, and suddenly every plan seemed like rubbish. Words tangled on his tongue. He surely must be sweating despite the cool of the evening. Some part of him had hoped she would realize the truth earlier, when she saw him dressed as the Bandit. He'd harbored a silly fantasy that some sort of surreal spark would fly between them and she would *know.* But she didn't.

I saw this going so much differently, he thought to himself. Now who had written a ridiculous Bandit episode? He had envisioned them sweeping around the ballroom with their grand secret, just as they had done about the Bible he hid in his pocket. They'd share a secret the whole world wanted to know, just the two of them.

He was about to give in and tell her when Stuart had plucked her from his grasp. Matthew had stood there, fuming on the dance floor for a few minutes, his great plan foiled. It was then that he came up with the idea of the note.

Surely now she'd come. This was a private part of the house, and no one from the party would be here. She'd know why the Bandit wanted to meet her. And then he could tell her. Ten long minutes from now. *Help me, Lord,* he pleaded as he pulled off his hat. *I'm twisted up enough as it is.*

He still had his hat in his hand when the French doors opened up and she came out onto the terrace. He gulped. So much for ten minutes.

She looked even more surprised than he. "Matthew!" she blurted, sounding much less pleased than he would have liked. "I…I found I needed some air." She put her hand behind her back. "I'll be fine in a moment. Please, don't let me keep you. Surely you ought to go and enjoy yourself at the party."

She was urging him to leave. Matthew's resolve wobbled a bit when he realized she truly had no idea he was the Bandit. It stung, but not enough to stop him. "Georgia…"

"I'll be back inside momentarily," she said, trying to look around casually. She was a charmingly poor liar. "It's a grand evening. I wouldn't want you to miss any of it."

The music of another waltz flooded out through the open doors. Matthew walked around her, noting how Georgia shifted her hand out of his view as he passed. She who kept many secrets was unskilled at deceit.

Instead of leaving, as he suspected she thought he was doing, he gently shut the doors. "Were you expecting someone?"

Her face twisted up just a bit, and the sight of it tied his heart in knots. "Well, I…" She was trying to lie, but couldn't bring herself to do it.

He laid his hat on the terrace table and pulled his mask off with the other hand. Somehow, as he removed it, every shred of doubt left him. He was, in every sense of the word, unmasking himself to her. "*I* was," he said softly.

She blinked, shaking her head just a bit. Her expression was so stunned, so transparent that he could watch her think. Watch the thoughts collide in her head. "No, really, I…"

He altered his voice to the one he had used as the Bandit. "I was expecting George."

Chapter Thirty-Seven

Georgia would have sworn an earthquake had just struck her back terrace. He? Expecting George? That could only mean…no. It couldn't be. He had somehow discovered the truth and had the audacity to toy with her so. Something close to anger swept through her.

She stared at him. "You couldn't…George…" The pieces began to fall into place. It was, in fact, completely possible. He'd told her he was good with voices as a child. As a visitor, he could move unrecognized throughout many parts of the city. The first strips of cloth had always been bandages from his arm. She'd just not seen it because she was embroidering every detail with her own fantasy.

"It is me," Matthew said, his gaze so fierce she thought she'd keel over. "It has always been me."

A thousand questions, a thousand thoughts tumbled in her head. The two men who held her heart were one man. Matthew was the Bandit. The Bandit was Matthew.

"H-how?" she stammered. "Why?"

He took a step toward her. "Mostly because it pleased you so. I saved Quinn by accident—it was happenstance that I was there. Then, when it appeared in the papers, I didn't know what to think. I didn't know you'd written the story. That first time, at Grace House, it was mostly because I knew you wished the Bandit to be true. I thought Stuart wrote about him as a gift of sorts to you. And, somehow, I knew I could make that gift come alive for you."

At first, it pained her as yet another manipulation. But looking at him, hearing his words and seeing the emotion laid bare in his eyes, she knew it truly had been a gift. "I begged you to tell me."

"It will be only a matter of weeks before I am called home. I thought it would hurt less if you did not know. If he remained unreal."

"And now?" Her voice wavered with the threat of tears. From pain or happiness, she couldn't yet say—they collided in the back of her throat.

"It hurt too much to keep deceiving you. It came to the point where even if I sailed tomorrow, I would bear it to give you one day of knowing it was me." He took another step toward her, his face suddenly dissolving into a look of vulnerability. "Can you not see it? How I care for you?" He swung his hands in a frustrated gesture. "I cannot bear to take you away from everything you love, and yet I cannot bear to stay away from you. I thought having the Bandit appear to you would solve it—that you could remain enamored of him in your mind and not suffer when I left." He stepped closer still and touched her cheek.

She brought her hand up to clasp his, and felt as if their

joined hands were the only thing keeping them from spinning off the end of the world. She tried to say something, but couldn't find words.

"But I could not bear it," he continued, the pain in his face slowly melting into a look of such tenderness that she was certain her knees would give way. "And, truth be told, I was jealous of your affection for him. I am your Bandit, Georgia. For as long as I can, I will do anything to save your world and make you happy."

The night careened around her. She could not draw in a breath deep enough.

He put his other hand to her cheek, so that he held her face. He stared at her as if she were the most precious treasure in all the universe. "Please say something," he whispered.

Georgia thought of all she had wished, the hero she had dreamed of, and the man she had resisted. She thought of Sister Charlotte's call to follow her heart, and God's call to her newfound courage.

Georgia Waterhouse became something she had never been: bold. And discovered that Sister Charlotte was indeed right—a wise woman *did* know a true kiss when it came her way.

Chapter Thirty-Eight

"You," Georgia said, when at last she pulled away. He nodded with a broad smile and sparkling eyes. "You," she repeated, still trying to grasp the wild idea.

"Do you find the concept so entirely implausible?" he teased. "I should like to think I am not entirely unheroic by daylight." He had the look of a man who had shed a great weight.

"I think you are a wonderful man, armed or unarmed." She couldn't resist. "But I must admit I did think your costume below par." She ran her hand down his arm, feeling the strength of his muscle as he held her. Delighting in the fact that it was *he* who held her. She touched the fabric of his shirt with wonder, as if it would give up clues to the adventures it had seen. "How amazing to discover it is in fact the real thing."

Matthew smiled, his eyes alight. "My hat has no mere nick in it, you know. Signore Trivolatti's meat hook is a most deadly weapon." He nodded as Georgia's fingers ran across the patch on his sleeve. "That came from those dreadful chickens."

"Oh," said Georgia, her head falling against his chest as the memory of the pandemonium made her laugh. "The chickens! Even Stuart enjoyed that chaos." She kept her head there, clinging just a bit tighter as the mention of her brother brought the world back into somber focus. "Does anyone know?" she asked, marveling when her cheek bumped up against a corner of what she knew to be Reverend Bauers's Bible.

"Bauers knows." Matthew stroked his palm down her arm, and she thought it the most soothing sensation in all the world. "He's been after me to tell you since Good Friday. He's been an accomplice of sorts." Matthew pulled back to look into her eyes. It seemed amazing to her that his could look so dark and so bright all at once. "My valet, Thompson," he said, "worked it out weeks ago, but I've no idea how. The clothing was his doing. He'd be insulted to know you found my costume inferior."

"Perhaps I should revise my comment to say it is more 'authentic.'"

Matthew smiled. "Who knows you are George?" he asked softly.

"Only Stuart. I believe most people suspect it has been Stuart all along."

"Oh, they do. I did." He fingered a stray lock of her hair, his smile broadening at the feel of it. "I imagine quite a few of them would be slack-jawed to discover the author's real identity. You would surprise quite a few people."

Which brought up the unwelcome subject of what to do

now. The world had spun on its ear not half an hour ago. How would the new world turn from here? She pulled away from his embrace and walked to the edge of the terrace. "Matthew, what do we do?"

He sat down on the short wall. "I am at a loss. Other than praying for legions of divine guidance, I hadn't thought it through any further than that."

Georgia sat down on the wall beside him. "Surely, God must have some sort of reason for all this."

"I can only—"

"Peach!" Stuart's voice came from behind the French doors. "Are you out here?"

Georgia's heart leaped into her throat. She shot up off the wall and rushed to the doors as she heard a rustle behind her. "Stuart?" She kept her hands firmly on the door latch, prepared to block it from opening with her foot if need be. When she turned and looked behind her, she was alone on the terrace. Matthew had somehow disappeared, but had left his hat and mask. "I'm out here," she said, as calmly as she knew how while she tossed the items over the wall into the bushes. "I needed some air." Stuart came though the doors. "All those Bandits."

"There's about a dozen you still haven't met yet. Have you spotted him?"

Georgia dreaded the prospect of having to lie to Stuart, so she was thankful when God gave her an answer that was indeed the truth. "I thought I would know him when I saw him."

"I'm sure you will. But you won't meet him out here, that's for certain."

Oh, Stuart, you have no idea how wrong you are. "It seems you'll have more introductions to make on my behalf, then."

"Actually, Peach," Stuart said as he undid the buttons on his frock coat and checked his watch, "I've got a bit of business to attend to. Can you manage on your own for a time? I won't be but half an hour, if that."

"Business, at this hour?" Georgia frowned at her brother.

"My presses never stop. Therefore my problems arise at all hours." It was a weak maxim Stuart quoted entirely too often.

"I am all too well acquainted with the notion," she replied. "Very well, do what you must. I'll be in the parlor searching out heroes."

Her brother's face darkened slightly. "Do find him, Georgia. I need to know who he is."

"So do I." She said a quick prayer that God would keep Stuart or anyone else from finding the hat and mask before Matthew did, and left Stuart to do whatever it was that needed doing "at all hours."

Matthew was doubling back for his hat and mask when he saw that the terrace was not empty. Stuart was pacing it, and there was no sign of Matthew's belongings. Georgia must have been clever enough to whisk them from sight in the nick of time. But why was Waterhouse out here when he had a houseful of guests to attend?

Matthew hung back in the shadows, watching. Stuart snapped his watch open and shut. Twice. He was meeting someone. Someone who was late, from the looks of his impatient frown. After a moment of two, Dexter Oakman walked out onto the terrace.

"Well," barked Stuart the minute Oakman had shut the French doors behind him. "What's the matter? I'm in the middle of something, if you hadn't noticed."

"There's a problem," said Oakman, taking a handkerchief from his pocket and wiping his balding forehead. It wasn't that warm an evening, something else was making him sweat.

"Well, I *gathered* there was a problem. I doubt you pulled me out here just to compliment me on the decorations." Stuart's voice took on a snarl Matthew had not heard before.

"There's a new policeman on the force. He's the problem I told you about before. We haven't been able to find a sufficient…incentive to get his cooperation. He'll be on the docks Thursday when the shipment comes in."

Incentive? Cooperation? Was Oakman talking about bribing someone? And whose shipment? Stuart's? He had his fingers in dozens of businesses around the city—importing could easily be one of them. Or, worse yet, were they discussing one of Covington Enterprises' own shipments?

"So offer him more money," Stuart replied, as if it were as simple as that. "It's taken me months to set this up. You know I can't afford to have this one go wrong. So find his price and pay it. Covington's got boxes coming in all the time. It shouldn't pose that big a problem, Dex." Stuart stared straight at Oakman, turning his back to Matthew in the process. From the look on Oakman's face, Stuart's expression must be deadly. "Your job is the easy part," he snarled. "Three hours. In the middle of the night, for that matter. Just get the opium off the boat and get Covington markings on the crates. Everyone suspects the Chinese, so no one's even looking our way." Stuart threw down a white ribbon he was holding and swore liberally. "Even my sister could do this. Get it done or I'll find someone else who can."

"I will," Oakman promised.

"Yes, you will. You will or it'll be the last thing you do for me. Now get out of here, and I don't want to hear about any more problems." He waved Dexter Oakman away and cursed a bit more as the man fled off through the French doors. Stuart stood alone on the terrace for a minute, fuming, before he snatched up the ribbon again and left the terrace, muttering under his breath.

Matthew pushed out a breath. Dexter Oakman and Stuart Waterhouse? Trafficking? It seemed impossible to believe. He'd always assumed the men were friends, but what he saw tonight was not friendship.

It all clicked into place within seconds. The funds moving in and out of the books at odd places—they were to and from Stuart. The extra personnel hid payoffs. And for as many crates that came onto the docks under the Covington stamp, a few more, for something as small and disguisable as opium, would slip by with ease. Stuart was right—everyone assumed opium the territory of the Chinese. No one would be looking for a well-bred white man to be trafficking against their powerful smugglers. Matthew imagined the Chinese thugs called "highbinders" would be quite nasty to Stuart should they discover him muscling in on their dealings.

Covington Enterprises had been corrupted.

What's more, Covington Enterprises had been corrupted by Dex Oakman working for Stuart Waterhouse. And who knew how many other Covington employees were under Stuart's thumb? There must be more than Oakman by now.

There'd be no end to the ugliness if this came to light. The weight of deceit Matthew had felt lifting off his shoulders just an hour earlier returned threefold.

His gut twisted. He'd just dispelled a lie, only to learn a far more gruesome truth.

Dear God, he cried out in the silence of his heart, *what do I do now?*

There were a dozen things he had to do. He had to get out of there and think—for a week, he guessed—about how to handle Covington Enterprises. He had to find a way to face Stuart Waterhouse calmly now that his stomach roiled in anger against the man—not to mention keep Dexter Oakman from suspecting he'd discovered something. He had to find a way to see Georgia again privately—although who knew what he'd say to her when he did. He had to go find Reverend Bauers and pray for guidance. He had to consult his father.

And all before Thursday. He sank down on his haunches at the base of a tree and shut his eyes. He'd read the story of Joshua and the walls of Jericho the other night. Another man facing an impossible challenge. *Could You please send one of those angels, Father? The army of the Lord would be rather handy right now.*

It had to start with Georgia. And it couldn't start with her unless he could see her. Bauers could arrange it more quickly than anyone. Tonight, even. Matthew hated to end tonight's happiness with such an ugly blow. Still, he had loved her enough an hour ago to give her the truth no matter the cost, and he would not stop now. She was like his Bible, he thought as he straightened up and put his hand over the book underneath his shirt. One could cut an enormous chunk out of her, and she'd still be able to do more good than most people. He just never thought he'd be the one wielding the knife.

Chapter Thirty-Nine

Reverend Bauers wandered out of his bedchamber with the look of someone growing weary of being roused by an Englishman at all hours of the night. He managed a weak grin when he saw that Matthew was still dressed as the Bandit—whip, sword and all. It was near one o'clock in the morning.

"I half suspected," Bauers said, yawning as he led Matthew into his study, "you'd come here tonight, but I thought you'd be glowing with happiness. You look dashing. And terrible." He stifled another yawn. "What has happened?"

"Everything," Matthew said, still working to keep the tidal wave of emotions from overtaking him. He slumped into a chair, planting his elbows on his knees and letting his head hang. He looked at his polished black boots and thought sourly, *I am no hero.*

Bauers pulled a chair up next to him. "I was so sure she cared for you. I am sorry."

Matthew looked up. "She does," he said, a cockeyed smile flitting across his face. "I am in love. It is dreadful."

The reverend looked puzzled. "I'll admit you have some rather unusual circumstances, but most men do look happier when they say such things. What happened?"

"She did not believe me at first. I thought she would know, somehow, just by looking at me, but even when I told her…it took a moment."

"You are the last person she would suspect," Bauers offered. "I imagine she's never had so great a surprise."

Matthew's heart turned over in his chest when he remembered the look in her eyes. "It was wonderful." He cast his gaze over to Bauers, who still appeared confused as to why a man who has just kissed the woman he loves seemed as if he were to be hanged within the hour. "And then it all fell to pieces."

"How?"

"We were almost interrupted by Stuart, but I managed to escape while Georgia held him off. I left my hat and mask, though, so I went back a few moments later. That was where I overheard Stuart and Dexter Oakman on the terrace." Matthew scrubbed at his face, trying to wipe away the fatigue suddenly flooding him. "I've been seeing trouble in the Covington books. Signs of wrongdoing, but nothing I could put a finger on. But it's them."

"What do you mean?" Bauers asked, still confused.

"Waterhouse and Oakman. They've been collaborating. Conspiring, actually. They've got a plan to traffic opium through Covington Enterprises. I believe the first shipment is to arrive Thursday night."

Bauers's face paled. "I find that hard to believe. Opium? Even Stuart would not fall in league with that lot."

"He's not," said Matthew darkly. "He's crossing them."

"Going against the highbinders? For opium? They'll have him killed."

"He wouldn't be the first." Matthew looked gravely at Reverend Bauers. "Or the last." He voiced the thought that had driven him here in the middle of the night. "They'd harm Georgia if they thought it would be the way to Stuart."

"I wish I could say you exaggerate. But I don't think you do." Bauers sighed heavily. "What ugliness. I do not think highly of Stuart Waterhouse, but even I would think him above this."

"The shipment must already be en route. We cannot stop it now. So the question becomes what do we do when it gets here?"

Bauers's expression echoed Matthew's thoughts: there were no good choices. Every option had terrible consequences. "The *true* question is what are you going to tell Georgia?"

It felt as if all Matthew's breath ran out of his body. "I must tell her. She needs to be part of whatever is decided."

Reverend Bauers looked relieved. "I am glad you see it that way." He leaned closer. "Still, can you not also see God's timing in this? It is no mistake that you are here, now, with her. That you were the one to discover this. Can you take heart from knowing this must surely be part of God's plan?"

"I should, but I'm finding it rather difficult to get past the disaster part. I do not care for the Lord's sense of timing on this."

Bauers put his hand on Matthew's shoulder. "I have a friend who once said that what we think of as disaster and calamity is often God's prelude to a mighty victory. After all, it takes a big problem to let God show how powerful He can be."

"In that case, I believe we qualify for a miracle." Matthew looked at the reverend. "Can you get her here? Now? Under some pretense?"

"Do you not think that a little rest might give you a clearer head? The dawn will not make things worse, but it might clear your thinking. You are welcome to stay here if you like, but perhaps you might want to get out of those clothes."

Matthew pulled himself off the chair and paced the room. "I'm exhausted, but I'm too angry to sleep. He's a weasel. A thoughtless, spineless snake without a moral to his name." He turned on the reverend. "What right does he have to take the Covington name down with him? To endanger Georgia? I have never been a man prone to violence, but so help me, Bauers..."

The reverend grabbed his arm. "All the more reason to put a little time behind you before you see Georgia. You've got to have your head about you when you tell her. You owe her that much."

Georgia woke to find her inkwell still open, her pen still lying atop the journal beside her on the bed. She'd written pages upon pages after retiring last night. The remainder of the party seemed a blur of unnecessary introductions, distracted small talk and secretive glances around the room. Part of her knew Matthew would be gone after their encounter on the terrace, yet part of her still surveyed the party on the slim chance he dared to stay.

Did he feel the way she did this morning? As if the world had begun turning in a new fashion? As if everything were too wonderful? Their circumstances had not changed; all the reasons why they could have little time together were still there. Yet when she thought of him and what it had felt like to settle into his strong arms last night, the obstacles seemed smaller. She knew one thing for certain: no matter what the future held, she would not have traded last night for all the world. Even though he did not know the half of what he'd done, Stuart had given her the most marvelous present ever. The fact that she would be presenting Reverend Bauers with a generous contribution later today was just God's overabundant blessing.

You knew all along, didn't You, Father? You knew he was there, but You knew the steps I needed to take to find him. The Bandit, the ball, I accomplished those things with the gifts You gave me. You've blessed me with courage and confidence, and rewarded me with love.

Love. Did she love him? Her heart answered with a cautious, exhilarated "yes." As if it felt too new to say for certain. She had loved parts of two men, knowing the impossibility of both. Now those two men had become one, and impossibility didn't seem…well, impossible. Did everyone newly in love feel as if nothing was beyond them? As if the combination of their hearts rendered all obstacles defeated?

England was still England. California was still California. Stuart, for that matter, was still Stuart. But Matthew was the Bandit. And that changed everything.

Georgia watched Matthew pull the door shut. Reverend Bauers's study was hardly a fitting place for such a meeting, but it was the most private, and inconspicuous, place possible.

Had Matthew been this handsome before? Surely he had not changed, yet Georgia could have sworn his eyes were a deeper blue, the cut of his shoulders broader, his voice smoother than yesterday.

He took her hand and kissed it as if it were the most precious thing God ever created. She'd rehearsed what she would say to him next time they stole a moment in private, and it came tumbling out of her at his touch. "I love you, and I don't care if you have to go back to England, because last night was enough for a lifetime and I love you for letting me know the truth." It came out in a gush of words, a single babbling exhalation that made her blush so fiercely she thought even the tops of her feet must be pink.

The resulting glow in his eyes surely turned her feet scarlet. He reached up and feathered his fingers against her cheek. He planted the tenderest of kisses where his fingers had been. It made her heart drop through her stomach.

"I had meant to be more elegant than that," she added when she could finally open her eyes. "But you seem to make my sense leave me."

Matthew circled her waist with his hands. "I don't know what future God holds for us, Georgia. Especially now. But I do know that I love you. I loved you even before you were George. I love you doubly now, and I would not take last night back for anything."

She'd thought, in her daydreams, that the moment they professed their love he would sweep her into a breathtaking kiss. She was sure of his words, but there was something dark lurking in his eyes, a tension in his face. "But what?" she said slowly, her intuition telling her all was far from well.

"But I do love you enough to offer you the truth," he continued, choosing his words carefully, "and there is something you must know. Something I only learned last night. A very hard truth, Georgia."

It seemed there should be something dramatic she should say. Something about drawing strength from love, or Paul's words about welcoming trials, but none of them fit the deeply pained way Matthew was looking at her. Something was very, very wrong.

"What is it, Matthew?" she asked, as steadily as she could.

He shifted his feet, glanced away for a second and then gazed straight into her eyes. *He's gathering courage,* she thought. *Whatever can be so awful now?*

"I have suspected for some weeks that all is not well at Covington Enterprises. Things have been…altered…for my arrival. Last night, after I left you, I discovered who has been planning crimes through Covington Enterprises and why." His hands tightened around her waist. He shook his head and groaned. "I do not know how to say this easily."

"Then simply say it," Georgia said, fighting her growing sense of fear. *He is leaving on the next ship,* she thought. *He's to be arrested within the hour. Men are plotting his murder and he needs to run for his life.* A thousand scenarios played out in her imagination. The horrible black hole in the pit of her stomach grew deeper with every look from him.

Matthew pulled in a shuddering breath. "The two men corrupting Covington Enterprises are Dexter Oakman and—and Stuart."

Chapter Forty

Georgia registered the names, but her mind would not accept the concept. "Stuart?" She stared at Matthew as he waited patiently for her to wade through the shock of what he had just told her. "Stuart?" she repeated. "He has no reason to. I don't understand."

"I came back for my hat and mask after I left you last night. Stuart was still on the terrace, evidently waiting for Oakman. I overheard their conversation. They are planning to smuggle in opium and hide it within the Covington shipments. They've been paying off port officials and policeman for some time, evidently, and that's what I've found hidden in the books."

Georgia pulled her hands from Matthew's. "Opium? The Chinamen's drug?"

"I gather there's a lot of money to be made in it. No one would suspect someone like Stuart. Or Covington Enterprises. Most consider it a purely Chinese affair."

"Stuart? Involved in something like that? No. Stuart is

misguided at times, but not this. Surely you misunderstood. Why ever would Stuart get involved? He's no friend of the Chinese, and certainly not their crimes. Those highbinders—I've heard enough about those. They…they *kill* people over far less than opium."

Matthew put his hand to his forehead. "I've no doubt they'd kill Stuart if he crossed them. Which, Georgia, is exactly what he is planning to do. Undercut the Chinese opium black market. He'd make a fortune—if he lives. Which I very much doubt he will, no matter how powerful he thinks himself to be. He's in danger, Georgia. Grave danger. Stuart's made enough enemies over the years. The highbinders would find him an easy target." He took her shoulders in his hands. "And, Georgia, you need to understand this. Listen to me. I fear they wouldn't hesitate to harm you to get to him. If Stuart fails Thursday night, he might pay for it in jail. But if he succeeds, then both of you are in danger. And Covington Enterprises is undone. Your world and mine could come apart Thursday night, and I do not know what to do about it."

It became hard to breathe. Stuart was cunning, unscrupulous, but this? This seemed beneath even him. His holdings were doing splendidly—what need did they have of more money? Such dangerous money? From such a horrible source? "It can't be true. Matthew, it cannot be."

He ran his finger down the angled edges of a pewter candlestick on the study shelf next to him. "I would give anything that it were not so." He looked at her, and she thought all the blue had fled his eyes, leaving them black and fathomless. He was afraid.

"Have you seen anything, heard anything, that might lead you to believe Stuart is up to something?" Matthew asked.

She looked at him—this man who was both a man and a hero—and felt her own fear ignite. Stuart had been acting strangely lately, and had indeed spent a lot of time with Dexter Oakman. He'd even started locking up his papers in a safe at night—something he had never done before. Could Stuart now be some stranger she did not really know? Some man capable of things she could not fathom?

"Perhaps. What do we do if it's true?" she whispered, clutching suddenly at his shoulder. "How can we save him? Or me?"

"I don't know how yet," he said, pulling her to him. She heard the frustration in his voice, felt the urgency tightening his chest. "But I promise you, if there's a way, we will find it. We," he repeated, tilting her face up to his. "You and me together. Between the four of us—you, me, the Bandit and George, there's got to be a way."

"Six," Georgia answered shakily. "I have a feeling we can count on Reverend Bauers and God as well." She attempted a small smile, but it failed miserably. Her lips melted into a pathetic, trembling pout.

He kissed away the tear that pooled at the corner of her eye. She felt small and defenseless, unable to keep up any semblance of courage. "Just when I thought I could not love you more," he whispered into her hair as he wrapped his strong arms around her, as if to keep the whole world at bay.

"Shut down the docks? We cannot simply shut down the port of San Francisco, Covington. It can't be done." Reverend Bauers, Georgia and Matthew sat around a table in the Reverend's study, supposedly factoring the Bandit Ball donations into Grace House's bookkeeping.

"I know that, Bauers, but we must find a way to effectively do that very thing."

"Or," mused Georgia, "focus so much attention onto the docks that the shipment can't go through unnoticed. Oh," she sighed, looking pained, "I hate this. I hate every single bit of it. I just can't believe Stuart's capable of something like this." Her voice quivered as she added, "He's my brother. My only family."

Matthew grasped her hand. "You have me. And I cannot begin to understand what it must feel like to be plotting Stuart's demise. But you must bear up, Georgia. You have it in you, I know you do."

"How can I go home? How can I pretend everything is fine when I know it is all going to pieces right in front of me?"

He wanted to wrap her up in his arms all over again. "Because you are strong enough," he said. "Because if Stuart suspects something it will be all the more difficult to seize the shipment." He stared hard into her eyes, willing her to feel the strength in herself that he had seen from the first. "You *are* strong enough." After a moment, he turned his gaze to Bauers. "We've got to paralyze the docks. Or at least slow the activity down substantially."

Georgia let her head fall into her hands. "Goodness, we'll need an army to do that."

Reverend Bauers suddenly froze. "And we know just how to raise one. Glory! I hadn't even thought of that."

"Bauers?" Matthew questioned.

"An army. I was thinking we needed an army to clear the

docks, but that's not it at all. We need an army to *fill* them. We've already done it once. It will be easy to do it again."

"Reverend?" Georgia said, looking as baffled as Matthew felt.

"Don't you see, Georgia? You called forth an army of Bandits for your ball. Hundreds of men dressed as the Bandit. They raised money because money *was what they had.* Now, call forth another army of Bandits for May Day, on Thursday. Call for a gathering of Bandits on the docks. They'll raise a ruckus because that's what *they* do. Think of it—the German tradition of the Maypole, all the ribbons—it's as good as if we planned it all along. If you issue an invitation through the *Herald,* the police will be primed to show up in heavy numbers. The docks will be swarmed and no will know who's who because there'll be so many Bandits."

"Are there that many German families here?" Matthew asked.

"Yes, but we don't have to stop there. You could write something to invite everyone. Irish families. Italian families. Even Chinese families. Turn it into a spontaneous May Day festival. They'll all have just finished reading about your Bandit Ball, and they're all ready to have a party of their own." Bauers reached across the table to take Georgia's hand. "You could do it, Georgia. You could write something to stir them up."

"I could very well start a riot," she replied.

"A riot might be the best weapon we have," Matthew answered. "It would both slow Stuart down and direct everyone's attention to the docks. I daresay it might work."

"How could I ever get something like that into the

Herald? Stuart would never run it. Not only that, if I somehow got him to, he'd know in advance and divert the shipment."

"Even if he knew in advance," Matthew retorted, "he has no way of diverting the shipment until the boat is already at the dock. In which case all he can do is keep it on board and delay its off-loading. We'd still be in a position to expose him."

"This is such a hideous business." Georgia stood up, her anger rising. Matthew had expected it to eventually find its way to the surface, and she was more than entitled to her feelings. She'd held out such hopes for Stuart. Persisted in believing the best of him, only to have it ripped out from beneath her. She paced the room now, her hands flailing in frustration.

"Exposing," she said bitterly. "Rioting. Why can't we simply go to the police with what we know? Why must it be so cloak-and-dagger?"

"Because we don't know who can be trusted," replied Reverend Bauers. "If Stuart's been buying off the officials for months, we've no idea who's in his pocket and who isn't." The clergyman rose and walked over to put a hand on Georgia's shoulder. "Try to think of it this way, child. If we expose Stuart, he'll suffer time in jail. If we don't expose him and he succeeds, eventually the highbinders will catch up with him, and I doubt their treatment will be anything as kind as jail. We are not exposing Stuart so much as saving him from himself."

"I'm done saving Stuart," she retorted, boiling over. Matthew was rather amazed that she'd lasted as long as she had. "Let him hang himself with his own greed." She pulled away from Bauers's grasp. "Who knows what else he's done? Who knows what sorts of awful things have been putting food on our table or buying my clothes or paying for silly balls! I've been a fool! A naive fool."

Matthew caught her arm as she stormed past him. "You've not been a fool. You have every right to be angry. And I admit, it's tempting to leave Stuart to his own fate. But you know you don't mean that. You're tired and upset and not yourself. Deserting Stuart is not who you are, even in anger. And aside from all else, it would put you in peril. I won't have that."

She turned to him, eyes blazing. "You won't have that?" He immediately knew he'd chosen the wrong words. "Isn't this *my* peril we're discussing?" she countered. "Shouldn't that be my decision?"

"Can't you see that perhaps I *am* here to protect you?" Matthew squared off in front of her. "That God brought me here, to you, to *see you safe?*" He took her by the shoulders, almost wanting to shake her despair out of her, surprised at his own panic that she might do something rash. "That He has made you so dear to me that I will do whatever it takes?"

He felt the set of her shoulders give just a little, and he pulled her to him, feeling her soften against his chest. "You've been betrayed by someone you love, and that's a terrible shock. But you are strong and clever. You've been saving San Francisco for years—do not stop now when it's yourself you must save." Her head fell against his shoulder and he planted a kiss onto her hair. "Go home. Plead a headache. Anything to keep to your rooms. I will ask Stuart to lunch or some such thing. Keep him occupied. He is no less a snake than many in London—I will be fine, even if I would like to wring his neck at the moment."

Matthew tilted her head to look into her eyes. "This is a part I can play. The part only you can do, Georgia, is to write Thursday's episode. Raise up our army. That is your gift. And now is the time to wield it."

Chapter Forty-One

Georgia felt ill. Sad. Furious. The emotions came so quickly she couldn't sort through them. *How amusing,* she thought to herself as she sprawled across her chair by the window. *I do remember once considering my life rather uneventful.*

Here she thought she had gained such courage over the past few weeks. Now, when it really mattered, when the storm of San Francisco's corruption showed up at her own doorstep, she was weak and frightened. She knew Stuart better than anyone. She knew what a ferocious enemy he could be.

Then again, she didn't know Stuart at all, did she? She thought she knew what he was capable of—but how sadly she'd misjudged how low he could sink.

Lord, help me! What am I to do? She remembered the story of Gideon, and fingered through her Bible to the sixth chapter of Judges. How she longed for an angel of the Lord to appear to her, to call her a mighty warrior and make her feel equipped for the task ahead of her. When Gideon asked,

"If the Lord is with us, why has all this happened?" she felt as if the ancient warrior was voicing her own thoughts.

Why, if God had indeed been instrumental in all the extraordinary things happening in her life, had it all unraveled so quickly? Gideon pleaded weakness. So did she. God promised to be with him, to help him conquer with the small strength he had. Oh, how she longed to claim that promise for herself. Gideon had named his altar, the spot he built to mark his encounter with the Lord, "The Lord is Peace." Gideon did not yet know how he was going to conquer his enemies. Yet he'd built an altar named for the Lord's peace. She could feel the words taking root in her heart. And when she read the final detail, one most casual readers would probably dismiss, she knew God had sent her comfort. Gideon, it seemed, was too afraid to do his tasks in the daylight—so he did them at night. Just like her Bandit.

Guide my pen, Lord, she prayed as she took her place at her writing desk. *Like Gideon, I am the least in my family and my enemies are great. My task is large. Be my mighty God, and do not leave my side for one second until I am through this.*

She dipped her pen into the ink and took a breath.

"People of San Francisco,
Let us find the heroes among us…."

"Grand of you to have lunch with me today, Stuart." Matthew shook his napkin open and signaled to the waiter to deliver the first course. He'd made sure they had the best table in the Palace dining room. Today, he was going to pull out every stop to monopolize Stuart's attention. In the time since he'd sent the invitation over and received Stuart's acceptance, he'd hatched a plan. It was extreme, rather risky, but Matthew doubted the circumstances called for anything less.

"Fine of you to ask. I'd been thinking we ought to chat, you and I." Stuart picked up a fork and surveyed his food. "You've been seeing a great deal of Georgia."

Ah, so he *had* been thinking along those lines. Matthew had suspected as much when Waterhouse agreed to the last-minute luncheon. "I have," he said, keeping his voice intentionally neutral.

"She's all I have in the world," Stuart stated.

It should have sounded sentimental. Instead, it sounded to Matthew entirely too much like the opening bid in an auction. He hid the twist in his gut and smiled genially. "She's a delightful woman. I find her talented and clever and of tremendous moral character."

"Oh, yes," replied Stuart, rolling his eyes the tiniest bit, "tremendous."

They ate for a few minutes, talking cordially, testing the waters as each waited for the true nature of the conversation to surface. When the second course had arrived, Matthew cleared his throat.

"Stuart," he said, leaning in, "I find you to be a direct man. I admire that, so I shall be direct as well. I find myself exceptionally fond of Georgia. I'd like to pursue her affections. I could give her a very comfortable life."

Stuart smiled. "I'm not entirely surprised, Covington. I know my sister well enough to see when a man has caught her eye." He cut into his chicken. "But I must admit, I hadn't thought things to have already grown that serious between you."

"These things," Matthew said with a wry smile, "do have a way of escalating." *Stuart Waterhouse, if you only knew the half of it.*

"Am I to understand you're declaring your intentions?"

"I am." Matthew reached for his glass. "I must admit, however, I've some doubts as to whether or not you'll let her go." He took a long drink, watching Stuart's reaction. "England is far away," he offered, "even with the railroad up and running."

"She's dear to me, Covington. I'll not have her hurt."

Not have her hurt? Have you given any thought to how you've placed her in danger just to stuff your coffers? It took a supreme effort of will to keep his voice cordial. "I think the world of her, Stuart. She'll want for nothing."

"Except me. I'll lose her to you. Do you deserve her?" her brother challenged.

Do you? It had been years since Matthew wanted to knock a man across a room as he wanted to this very moment. "Will you let her go with your blessing?"

Stuart wiped his mouth with his napkin, making a show of considering the offer before him. "The idea has merit. Can you prove to me she'll be well cared for?"

Matthew had anticipated this kind of thrust and parry, and he had a strategy prepared. "I'm prepared to place the San Francisco holdings of Covington Enterprises in Georgia's name as an engagement gift. I'll send for the papers tomorrow if you give me your consent to the marriage." It was just the sort of offer Stuart couldn't refuse—an importing firm in the family name. As such, it made the ideal setup for the final strike Matthew had planned.

"Does Georgia know of this?" Stuart asked, stalling his answer with another question. The man was shrewd, Matthew gave him that.

"I believe I know Georgia's heart. But I would not approach her about this until I'd spoken with you. As a matter of honor."

Stuart waited a full minute more before extending his hand. "Very well, then, Covington, it seems we are to be family."

Matthew couldn't think of a more disturbing thought. "Covington Enterprises will be hers by the month's end. On one condition."

Stuart's brows shot up. "'Condition'? Rather unconventional, wouldn't you say?"

"You strike me as a man who understands a deal, Waterhouse."

"That depends on the deal." Stuart crossed his arms over his chest, looking intrigued and not a little annoyed.

"I know more than you think I do, Stuart." He lowered his voice. "I know, for example, who George is."

Chapter Forty-Two

Stuart went very still. He stared at Matthew before saying, "Go on."

"I value her role in that, because I value that part of her. So, if I'm to place my family holdings in her name—and within your family—I want to know you value it as well. I've declared my pledge. I only want one thing from you in return."

"Not really your place to bargain, is it, Covington?"

"It's simple, really. No effort from you at all. I just want your promise to run the Bandit episodes verbatim. Just as Georgia writes them, no editing. If she's to finish out her run as George Towers, then I want her to have the freedom to do it as she pleases. *Exactly* as she pleases."

"That's it?" Stuart balked. "That's what you want?"

"It's important to her, therefore it's important to me. I've read the latest installment, so I'll know if it's been altered in any way when it appears in print on Thursday." He held out a hand. "Have we a deal, Stuart?"

"Is this how brides are won in England?" Confound him, Stuart was stalling to the end.

"It's how *this* particular bride is *wooed.* Do we have a deal?"

Stuart shook his hand. "Done."

"I'm grateful. I'll speak to her tomorrow night, if that suits you. You'll have your papers by Monday if I can manage it."

Stuart gripped Matthew's hand a moment longer. "She's all I have in the world, Covington."

"She's worth the world to *me,* Stuart. I hope you see that."

"Believe it or not," he said, with a smile that could be described as warm—if one did not look too carefully, "I think I do."

Georgia could barely wait to get out the door with Matthew the following afternoon. The air in the house felt thick with secrets, and it seemed like hours before he came to call. Adventure and intrigue were clearly ideas best left to the printed page, and not one's own family. She'd avoided Stuart all day yesterday, and he had been looking at her oddly today. It added to her nerves when she handed him the fateful Bandit episode over lunch. Odder still, he accepted it without a single question—not reading it then, as he usually did, and as near as she could tell not reading it at all.

Sensing that an "outing" was not really suited to their moods, Matthew suggested they simply take a walk. It was a fine afternoon, and he led her to the set of benches where he had first read the Bandit to her. The slanting gold sunlight brought a deep sapphire to his eyes. He sat down opposite her, looked at her, then stood up again.

Nervous, she realized. *He's nervous.* She'd never seen

him nervous. Alarmed, yes. Agitated. But never nervous. She wondered if something had gone very wrong with his meeting with Stuart. "Matthew," she began, at the exact same moment he said her name. They both blustered a bit, and then he gestured for her to continue.

"What have you said to Stuart? He has been acting strangely all day, and he took my Bandit episode without so much as a peep. I'm not even sure he's planning on reading it before he hands it to the typesetter. How did you do it?"

"Yes, well," said Matthew, with the tone of voice one uses when starting a long speech, "I've been meaning to speak to you about that." He thrust his hands into his pockets, only to remove them again, and sat down. "Georgia, do you remember the verse you read to me? The one from Corinthians?"

"Of course," she replied.

"It speaks of having everything, but of it all coming to nothing without love."

"Yes, it does."

"I...I don't find it any accident that that was the verse you shared with me. It's had a great impact on me." He turned to look at her. "You've had a great impact on me."

She wanted to reply that he'd changed her as well, but something told her to stay silent, to let him finish whatever he needed to say.

"I have a great many things. I own more than I can ever use, I have more influence than I can ever hope to wield wisely, and—" the spark in his eyes traveled to ignite his wide smile "—I have gained faith and friends I would never have imagined. But I had not love until I met you. I understand now what those verses mean, because all the things I have, the things I am, pale in comparison to love." He took her hand. "I have come to love you. Dearly. And yet I cannot tell you what our future will be. I find I can't even predict how the week will end."

Had he said "our future"? Georgia suddenly realized what he was doing, why his nerves were so wound up, and she fought to pull in a breath.

"Yesterday morning, I sat in my rooms and begged God to show me what to do. He did, Georgia. He gave me a plan so perfect and so impossible that I knew at once how to proceed. But here, now, is not about any plan. It is not about how useful this tactic is. It is about how I cannot see myself without you, no matter what the circumstances."

She wasn't quite sure what he meant, talking about tactics and such, but she could see an astounding intensity in his eyes.

He took her hands. "Yesterday I asked Stuart for his blessing to marry you. I want to marry you, Georgia Waterhouse, and I don't care how impossible it all sounds right now." He gave a sheepish laugh, something so out of place in his usually confident demeanor. "I don't even know how I'll manage it yet. I don't know any of the details—here or England or family or any of it." His hands tightened around hers. "But I know it is what I want. More than anything. And I think…no, I *believe*…God has a life together planned for us. If you'll have me."

Georgia understood his words. She knew what he was saying. Yet it felt as if someone had just hit her with a thousand sparks of light. "You're…you're asking me to marry you."

He pulled one hand away and raked it through his hair.

"Well, I admit to being rather long-winded, but yes." He took her hands again and stared into her eyes. Oh, what the blue-black depths of them did to her. "Georgia, I am asking you to marry me. Will you?"

She had told herself over and over that it could not be. That it wasn't really what she wanted, for it might mean leaving San Francisco. She'd given herself all manner of sensible reasons why their happiness would only be a fleeting thing. Nothing to grasp at. But here, now, she wanted to grab it with both hands and hold it close forever. She wanted to be with Matthew, and the future would have to be God's problem to contend with as He chose. There wasn't even a moment's hesitation to her answer. She realized that no matter how she'd deceived her more sensible self, she'd said yes to a future with him a long time ago.

"You?" she said, knowing he'd already seen her acceptance in her eyes, "or the Black Bandit?"

He grinned. "The whole lot of us."

"Yes," she said breathlessly. "Yes, I will."

Forgetting they were in the middle of a park, he pulled her into a recklessly long kiss. "I've no ring yet," he said, when they found their wits again. "You'll have a fine one in time, but for now, I think perhaps I've found a suitable proxy." Fumbling in his pocket, he pulled out a tiny white ribbon and tied it around her ring finger, finishing off with a kiss to her hand. "A fitting token for our most unusual courtship, don't you think?"

"I don't know how on earth we'll manage it," she agreed, touching the tiny bow, "but we've managed quite a lot of the impossible so far. Perhaps we stand a chance. Goodness, if

Stuart agreed and ran the Bandit without question, God must be on our side."

"Yes, well, there's something I have to tell you about that. But I needed to hear your yes first before I let you in on my agreement with your brother."

"Your agreement," she repeated, feeling a bit unsteady, "with Stuart?"

"I'll admit at first I thought it only a tactic. But I think that is purely how God got my attention. I think it might have taken me months to work up the nerve otherwise."

"Matthew, what are you talking about?"

"I told Stuart I would transfer Covington's San Francisco holdings into your name—something I knew he'd find irresistible—as an engagement gift. On the condition that he run your future Bandit episodes without any editing whatsoever. He knows I know you're George. And I told him I'd seen the present Bandit installment, so you'd best show it to me quickly so I can verify he's kept his end of the deal."

"A deal? You struck a deal with Stuart? For me?" She eyed him.

"I struck no deal for you, Georgia. I want to marry you. God just had to knock me over the head to realize it. But I'll admit to playing my present desires to our best advantage. It works beautifully. Your Bandit episode will run in the *Herald* now, and our plan stands a greater chance of succeeding. But please, know it is only a happy consequence of what I truly want—which is for us to be together."

Georgia sighed. "I cannot see how it is at all possible. One of us should have to leave everything."

"I made it here. The railroad is growing every day. Each

ship built is faster than the last. Perhaps the world is not as large as it once was. I believe we will find a way. Perhaps, Georgia, God is paving the way for a new life for you. Whether it is here or in England, I don't know. We'll have to deal with that as it comes. But if Stuart is brought down, can you not see that perhaps God is clearing the way for you to go to England? Or at least granting us that possibility?"

She let out another sigh. "I don't know."

"You and the reverend won me to faith with half a Bible. You created a hero out of thin air. The Bandit has worked wonders and still no one knows who he is. I've been stabbed by an Irishman, stitched by a German, costumed by an Englishman, conspired with an Italian and loved by an American. I believe the small matter of a few continents and an ocean is well within our means."

Chapter Forty-Three

The world seemed to grind to a halt until Thursday. Georgia nearly ran to breakfast Thursday morning, eager to see the Bandit episode printed in the *Herald.* It appeared exactly as she had written it. If Stuart suspected anything or was annoyed with her call for an impromptu celebration on the docks that night, he showed none of it. As a matter of fact, he was up and at the offices long before she even woke. She laid her hand over the newsprint and prayed. *Send these words out in Your name, Father. Let Your will be done today. Raise up a throng to fill the docks, and let the police find what they need to find.*

Her heart constricted as she contemplated Stuart's fate by this time tomorrow. *Is there no way to save him from this, Lord? Turn him back from this mistake, I beg You. Can You not see Your way clear to a fate that is neither prison nor the highbinders? Can You not work a miracle?* Her soul fell upon the words she'd so long resented from Stuart: *he's all I have in the world.*

* * *

Matthew thought it would be far more difficult to locate the boxes. As head of Covington Enterprises, he found it easy to gain access to the ship's manifest when it docked. Within an hour, he'd managed to sort out a dozen or so likely crates from the legitimate cargo. Then, by discreetly watching the unloading, noting how each crate was handled and by whom, he had narrowed it down to six by the end of the day. He had his target. Matthew went home to get ready, the first part of his role done. Now it was up to Bauers to direct the crowd Georgia had summoned.

As evening fell and he pulled on his boots, Matthew took a moment to run a finger across the glossy leather. How odd that he had to hide in a sea of Bandits tonight in order to drop that persona forever. He looked up at Thompson, who seemed to understand the irony of the moment. "I won't be home tonight, Thompson. Not till daylight at best."

"I gather the Bandit is facing a great challenge this evening, sir?" There was no hint of teasing in the valet's voice.

Matthew thought of all the times throughout his life he'd kept things from Thompson, tried to outwit him. It struck him that today might be the time for a new tactic—to tell Thompson everything. To allow him to be the ally he had always quietly been. Without saying a word, Matthew got up, poured two cups of coffee from the service on the sideboard and added two sugars to one—that was how Thompson took his coffee. He offered it to him, a gesture of service to the man who had so faithfully served him.

Thompson seemed to understand what Matthew was doing, and offered a rare, wide smile. "Thank you, sir."

"Matthew. Just Matthew will be fine."

"Thank you...Matthew."

He sat down opposite the valet, and they sipped their coffee in silence. "Covington Enterprises has been corrupted," Matthew began. "Stuart Waterhouse is planning to smuggle opium into the country through our shipments, beginning tonight. Waterhouse is taking on the highbinders, powerful Chinese smugglers, and trying to undercut them. To his danger and Georgia's." He looked into Thompson's face. "I care a great deal for Georgia Waterhouse."

The valet set down his cup. "I have been waiting a long time for you to find someone, Mr. Cov...Matthew. I believe you have chosen exceptionally well."

Matthew managed a lopsided grin. "Does one really choose such things?"

"No," replied Thompson, "I suppose they come upon us—even when we would have chosen otherwise." He sighed, taking another sip of coffee. Matthew remembered that Thompson had been married once. His wife had died several years earlier. Had Matthew ever truly paid attention to his grief, or just assumed that the man's service would simply endure, at it always had?

"Waterhouse—and Covington Enterprises—will be exposed tonight. It will be an ugly evening for all of us, Stuart most of all. I doubt this division of the company will survive the month, either. I'm sorry for that."

"Your father will not be pleased," Thompson agreed. "But Covington Enterprises has many holdings. The fall of one office will not bring down so vast an empire."

"So vast an empire," Matthew echoed, the enormity of the evening pressing down upon him.

"The Bandit is a clever man. I believe he can manage it." Thompson caught his eye with a strangely confident look. "And she is worth it."

Matthew found himself sharing Thompson's smile. "Yes, she most certainly is."

While she knew it was the least dangerous, Georgia felt as though she had the most difficult task of all: keeping Stuart occupied. Even sharing the happy news of her engagement to Matthew—which provided her a bevy of small details to "pretend" the need to discuss—it was as though she and Stuart were different people. No longer the lone siblings. At first, she thought it was because Matthew had entered that very private circle, but she recognized that deceit had been the true invader.

What had come between them was not Matthew, but Stuart himself.

"What fun you shall have with new British relatives!" she said too cheerfully. "I imagine several of Matthew's family will share your love of operetta."

"They might at that," said Stuart, also grasping at conversation. He checked his watch again.

"Crisis at the presses tonight?" she inquired stiffly.

"Isn't there always?" he answered with another question—a sure sign he was on the defensive. Georgia pretended to be engrossed in her embroidery, praying for God's sovereignty with each distracted stitch. It would be so long a night.

Still, she had come to a significant realization today: this was about more than Stuart and his faults. Today—in fact for many weeks now—she was discovering how to be Georgia Waterhouse. Not merely "the other Waterhouse," or "Stuart's sister." God was granting her the gift, however painful, of becoming her own person.

Such a gift took courage of a whole other kind to receive. Not the courage of sword or whip or strength in the face of danger, but one of trust and faith and confidence. No matter what transpired tonight, none of those blessings would be taken away. Challenged, perhaps, but they were hers now, and could no longer be stolen from her. Not even by Stuart.

When she looked up from her stitches, Stuart was staring at her. "Do you love him, Peach?" he asked in a tone that tightened her throat. "Really?" The old Stuart, the wild, misguided, big-hearted child returned in his eyes.

Suddenly, for the first time ever, Georgia felt older than her brother. As though she had grown in a way he never had. Stuart had loved once—fallen madly in love—but it was always a possessive sort of craving with him. It seemed a shallow echo of what she felt for Matthew. A tinge of pity stole into the mixture of fear and anger she'd felt since she'd learned of his plans.

"Yes," she said. "Very much." And there, right there, was faith working itself out in her life. Faith giving her the strength to love when it was not deserved. Faith enabling her to love the sinner, yet hate the sin. Faith to grasp her life apart from Stuart, to release him to his fate, and yet still love him. "Thank you," she said sincerely, "for extending your blessing. It means a great deal to me."

"We're all we have in the world," he said, nearly hiding the hint of sadness in his eyes.

No, she thought, *there's where you're wrong.*

Matthew waited outside Dexter Oakman's house until the man left around ten o'clock. While Stuart would never sully his hands with the actual dirty work, Matthew had seen him apply enough pressure that he suspected Oakman would personally oversee the transfer. Sadly enough, the man who would come out the worst for all of this was Oakman. Stuart might have the finances and wit to recover one day, but Matthew doubted Oakman would ever regain any position whatsoever.

He followed Oakman's carriage down toward the docks and Covington Enterprises. The closer they got to the shipyards, the noisier the streets became. Bauers, who had always been resourceful, must have outdone himself, for the area was packed with loud, raucous people, many dressed as the Bandit. Slipping into the crowd, Matthew became instantly invisible. *Thompson, old man, I've finally mastered it,* he thought to himself, tipping his black hat in the general direction of the Palace Hotel.

Policemen were trying desperately to keep some semblance of order. If there was one thing this part of the city did well, it was raise a ruckus. Put the crowd in masks, add a generous amount of ale and inspiration, and it quickly turned into May Day chaos. In the three-block radius around Covington Enterprises, Matthew saw more policemen than he had witnessed during his entire visit.

He flattened himself against a wall as Oakman met up

with two men. *Come on now, Dexter, come take your precious present home from the party.* Matthew looked around to make sure there were plenty of policemen in view. Carefully, with a few nervous glances, Oakman motioned for three of the half-dozen crates Matthew had suspected to be loaded onto a wagon.

What Oakman and his men did not know was that Matthew had loosened the bottom of each of those crates so that they would come loose when lifted. The string of curses let out when the first crate collapsed would have burned Georgia's ears. A rainbow of Oriental silks spilled out onto the street. An expensive mistake, but it confirmed Matthew's suspicion that the opium had been hidden inside something like fabric or fiber.

The mishap caught the attention of a few of the policemen, who made snide remarks about the careless nature of dockworkers.

The second crate caved in the instant it was lifted, signaling it contained more than just fabric. Sure enough, small paper parcels rolled out of their silk cocoons and sent Oakman into a panic. Now was the time.

Matthew lit the fuse on a firecracker wound with a wad of cotton he had purchased earlier, and tossed it into the center of the pile. The sound, one of many firecrackers going off in the melee, brought little attention. The flare, however, sent the cotton up in flames, which ignited the silk—a slower fire that resisted stamping out. It in turn ignited the real target by the time the police gathered. The pile began to give out the thick, musty odor every San Francisco policeman knew as opium smoke.

The scene reminded Matthew of the passage in his namesake's gospel where Christ said He would separate the sheep from the goats. Within the space of a minute, the police force divided itself squarely into men trying to cover things up and men trying to find things out. Pulling off his mask and hat, Matthew stepped into the light and headed straight for the latter.

Chapter Forty-Four

"I'm Matthew Covington," he said to the one who appeared to be in command. "I've discovered this man trying to smuggle opium into the port through my shipping, and I want him arrested along with his accomplice, immediately."

Dexter Oakman went white. The scent of opium smoke hung in the air as he stared at Matthew.

"I'm Sergeant Dickenson, Mr. Covington." The officer extended a hand. "And what do you mean by accomplice?"

Matthew pulled a roll of ledger papers—unaltered ledgers he'd managed to dig out of some back files at his office after considerable searching—from one of the pockets of his trousers. "A quick study of these should point straight to Stuart Waterhouse. You'll find him at home awaiting a report from our friend here."

Dickenson briefly riffled through the papers. "I'll have to get someone to look at these more closely, but this is a serious charge, Mr. Covington. I wouldn't make it lightly."

"Nor do I set fire to my own cargo lightly, Dickenson.

This was to be the first shipment Waterhouse smuggled in, but I gather with a little digging you'll find a host set to come in behind it. I've marked the involved transactions in these ledgers here. I'm prepared to cooperate fully with your authorities and open up all of Covington's books to your perusal. But I've found many of my books to be altered. And I guarantee you, Waterhouse will disappear within the hour if you don't move quickly."

Several other policemen, the ones in obvious disagreement with Dickenson's planned course of action, came up behind them as they spoke. "I hope you know what you're saying, Covington," the sergeant warned. "Waterhouse is not a man to count among your enemies."

"I know full well what I'm saying."

Dickenson motioned to two of his colleagues. "You two, go bring in Stuart Waterhouse for questioning." They looked as though they'd been asked to wrestle a cobra with their bare hands, but they went. "You'll need to come with me, Covington. Highly unusual, what you're doing."

"You don't want to do this," snarled a burly older officer from behind Dickenson's shoulder. "You might want to think this over if you like yer job."

Dickenson caught Matthew's eye before turning to the man. "And you might want to think about what you've just said in front of a witness like Mr. Covington here. Just in case any of it might happen to be true. Which I'm not saying it is. I'm sure Mr. Waterhouse will be eager to tell us his version of the facts—" he returned his gaze to Oakman "—but for now we gotta put out this fire. Nasty smellin' stuff, it is."

Dickenson's glower put Oakman in a panic. "Matthew,"

he said, pulling against the pair of policemen who had just taken him by the elbows, "don't. We'll lose everything."

"I've lost nothing of real value," Matthew replied.

Dickenson glanced again at the papers, holding them up to a gaslight in the corner. "You realize what you're doing? You ready to tangle with Waterhouse? It could get just as nasty for you. We can stop at your friend here."

"I'm quite certain, Sergeant. It's a matter of some personal consequence to me."

Dickenson sighed like a man who had just resigned himself to a very nasty fight. "I been waiting for something like this to crawl its way up to Nob Hill. Like my mama used to say, it ain't just cream that rises to the top—grease does, too."

"Matthew," called Oakman, "think of your family."

"I am," he said calmly. *The one I will someday start with Georgia.*

"You've a long night of questioning ahead of you, Covington," said Sergeant Dickenson, tucking the papers into his coat pocket, "if we can carve our way through the sea of Bandits." He pointed to the full-scale calamity enjoying itself farther up the dock. "Nice Bandit costume, by the way. You must have had a good time at Waterhouse's ball, though—it looks a mite ragged around the edges."

When Matthew rang the bell, Reverend Bauers opened the front door of the Waterhouse estate. The sun was just coming up. Bauers shook his hand heartily, then led him to the front parlor, where Georgia was dozing on the settee. She held a handkerchief with the initials SW embroidered on one corner in her hand.

"He's going to be all right, Georgia," Matthew said when she opened her eyes, thinking it was what she needed to hear.

"No," she said, pulling herself upright, "he won't. But God is wise and kind, and no less God than He was yesterday." She looked at him, rumpled and dirty in his Bandit costume. Her gaze traveled to his waist. "You've lost your whip. And your hat—where is your hat?"

Matthew smiled. "I gave them to Quinn. My mask as well. I wanted to say thank-you to him. You should have seen him, stirring up the crowd. Besides, I won't be needing them anymore."

"No more Bandit adventures? Matthew, whatever shall we do now?"

"I'm afraid I haven't the foggiest idea. Can you live with that?"

She smiled. "I imagine George and I can find a way." She stood up and adjusted his collar, running her hand across the stubble on his chin. "Tell me, what do they eat for breakfast in England?"

Epilogue

London Times
"Madam Whippleton's Most Delectable Social Gossip"
May 2, 1892

London's finest were decked out in their swashbuckling best last night as Mr. and Mrs. Matthew Covington hosted what is sure to become a fixture in the spring social calendar. The First Annual May Day Bandit Ball, said to be a quaint tradition brought over by Mrs. Covington from her native California. The gala event raised funds to support the Willsbury Home for Orphaned Children, a most worthy cause that has been a focus of Mrs. Covington's since her arrival here two years ago. Festive touches such as a cascade of white ribbons and a traditional German Maypole added to the theatrical atmosphere of the evening. London's finest joined in the spirit of the costumed event, making generous philanthropic gifts for the privilege of dressing as Robin Hood, Aladdin, the Three Musketeers, Blackbeard the Pirate, or any number of legendary bandits throughout the ages. Good show, Mrs. Covington—this author, for one, delights in your spirited contribution to London's stoic social offerings.

Now, on to the loathsome qualities of Miss Edwina Dyson's gown at the opera last Thursday. Surely someone should speak to her seamstress...."

* * * * *

Dear Reader,

Those of us who write can't help but imagine what the world would be like if our characters came to life—especially one as handsome and heroic as Matthew. Sometimes, in our pursuit of an idealistic dream, it's easy to miss the heroes right in front of us every day. I hope MASKED BY MOONLIGHT not only entertained you for a few hours, but made you think about what's possible in our real world and in the people around us. Not to mention what's possible within ourselves. We serve an amazing God who can do astounding things with ordinary people—and I believe that provides us with the best adventure of all.

And if you're wondering what Quinn's going to do with that mask, well, let's just say I'm hoping you won't have to wait too long to find out….

As always, I love to hear from you at www.alliepleiter.com or by mail at P.O. Box 7026, Villa Park, IL 60181.

Blessings,

QUESTIONS FOR DISCUSSION

1. If you could create a heroic alter ego for yourself, what would she/he be like?

2. Was Matthew right to step into the Bandit persona? What would you have done in his "boots"?

3. Is your faith journey more like Matthew's or Georgia's? What are the differences and how do they affect your journey?

4. Why do you think Georgia could continue to put up with Stuart for so long? What made her able to pull away from him when she did? Was it the right choice?

5. Reverend Bauers quotes, "What we think of as disaster and calamity is often God's prelude to a mighty victory." Where in your life has that proved to be true?

6. If you were Reverend Bauers, would you have helped the Bandit? Why or why not?

7. Think about an everyday hero you know. What can you do to recognize him or her?

8. Georgia sympathizes with Gideon's plea, "If the Lord is with us, why has all this happened?" Have you ever felt that way? What can you do about it?

9. Why do you think God sent Matthew into this circumstance? What about Georgia? What makes them such a perfect match for the challenges at hand?

10. If you were Matthew, when would you have told Georgia you were the Bandit? Does your choice differ with Matthew's choice in the book? Why?

11. Play author yourself for a moment. What do you think will happen to Stuart? Is he a redeemable character?

12. If you, like Georgia, were asked to read your favorite Bible verse to someone, which would you choose? Why?

Love Inspired
HISTORICAL

TITLES AVAILABLE NEXT MONTH

Don't miss these two stories in July

HIGH COUNTRY BRIDE by Jillian Hart
For widow Joanna Nelson, life presented constant hardships. Evicted from her home, she and her two children sought refuge on rancher Aidan McKaslin's property. He sheltered her family, while she brought faith and a woman's touch back into his world. Could Aidan convince the special woman to bind herself to him permanently or would he drive her away forever?

SEASIDE CINDERELLA by Anna Schmidt
Nantucket Island offered Lucie McNeil a chance for a better life. But her quiet existence was thrown into chaos when her employers' handsome son stepped ashore. Their pasts were connected by tragedy. She knew she should hate Gabriel Hunter, yet she could not. Instead she was drawn to the caring soul she sensed behind the ruthless facade he showed the world.

LIHCNM0608